Sharp Sticks, Driven Nails

SHARP STICKS DRIVEN NAILS

An anthology of new stories edited by
Philip Ó Ceallaigh

The Stinging Fly

A Stinging Fly Press Book

Published October 2010

The stories by Alex Epstein are from *Blue Has No South* translated by Becka Mara McKay
(Northampton, Mass: Clockroot Books, 2010). Grateful acknowledgement is also made
to *The Iowa Review*, where two of these five stories first appeared. Reprinted with permission.

Set in Palatino

The Stinging Fly Press
PO Box 6016
Dublin 8
www.stingingfly.org

ISBN: 978-1-906539-15-3

The Stinging Fly gratefully acknowledges funding support from
The Arts Council / An Chomhairle Ealaíon and Dublin City Council..

'Then I began to speak of style, of the army of words, an army in which all kinds of weapons are on the move. No iron can enter the human heart as chillingly as a full stop placed at the right time.'
—Isaac Babel, from 'Guy de Maupassant'

'The words of the philosophers are as sharp sticks, their assembled proverbs as lasting as firmly driven nails.'
—*Ecclesiastes*, 12:11

CONTENTS

INTRODUCTION

Short stories are born of the ambition to see life in a new way, to reveal it, perhaps to endow experience with the clarity or sense that it lacks in the middle of the untidy business of living. But whether a writer revisits experience playfully or seems be under a terrible pressure to redeem it, a short story, being short, presents itself modestly. The ambition is hidden.

This is the paradox. The short story demands the concision and accuracy we associate with poetry, while using all the modalities— place, character, progression, drama—we associate with more sprawling narrative forms. And yet it has to come off naturally and gracefully, like any practised art, showing no sign of the work.

The twenty-two authors represented here are from eight different countries. Some are established writers, others are relative new-comers. Some are joking around, others are deadly serious. Their stories vary vastly in theme and style. Some of them, certainly, show more ambition than others. But if I have to point to something that unites these stories, that made me want to include them here together, it is that they display the freshness and clarity that comes of rendering something simple.

Put another way, these stories struck me as pieces of extraordinary good luck. They appear unlaboured. The trick seems effortless.

And that is as it should be.

—Philip Ó Ceallaigh
Bucharest, August 2010

Sharp Sticks, Driven Nails

WAITING FOR THE BULLET
MADELEINE D'ARCY

My husband Turlough arrived home with the gun a few weeks ago. I heard him coming in from work and putting his laptop on the hall table as usual, then the sound of packaging being ripped open as he strode into the kitchen. Turlough's an immediate presence, full of energy. When I first met him this thrilled me, but lately it makes me feel—not tired exactly—maybe just a little diminished.

'Look at this!' he said. 'It's brilliant.' He threw the gun onto the worktop. It was made of metal and the butt was beige-coloured plastic.

'Jesus!' I said.

'Ah, cop yourself on, Melissa. It's only a toy.' He picked it up, pressed something and the barrel fell open. 'Look, this is how you load it.'

He took a red plastic circle from a tube, pushed it into the exposed cylinder and clicked it shut. Then he pointed the gun at my face and pressed the trigger. The sharp crack of the gunshot sounded so real that I ducked. A haze of smoke hung in the air and behind it Turlough laughed.

'You should see your face! Isn't it convincing?'

'It's horrible,' I said.

'Ah, it's only a bit of fun.'

'Let's put it away,' I said. I shoved it into the junk drawer and began to make dinner.

*

The junk drawer is part of an ugly armoire that my mother-in-law gave us. 'It's an heirloom,' she said, but I suspect she was yearning to get rid of it. If I could, I'd junk the entire piece of furniture. There's one big drawer at the base, and that's where I put stuff destined for the charity shop or the dustbin—things I can't throw away immediately, usually because they belong to Turlough.

That night, while Turlough was out playing tennis, I contemplated the contents of the junk drawer. The first thing I saw was a cigarette lighter shaped like a woman with 'Souvenir of Lanzarote' engraved on it—it was about time I got rid of that. Among various other useless objects, there was a Casio pocket viewer (unused since he got his Blackberry) and a candy-striped tie from Brown Thomas that made him look like a pimp. The gun was there too, nestling between a packet of condoms in the colours of the Irish flag and a key-ring with a plastic pint of Guinness attached. I took the gun out and became oddly fascinated by it. I loaded it, aimed at the fridge and shut my eyes, then pressed the trigger. The sound was loud and convincing.

I fired six more times, aiming through the window at birds and a stray cat, until I hardly jumped at the noise any more. Finally, I looked in the mirror and shot myself in the head. As I put the gun away, I felt strangely fulfilled.

I was reading in bed when Turlough lurched in.

'Night,' he said as he lowered himself into bed and turned on his side. I moved close to him but he didn't turn around, just said, 'You haven't forgotten that Stacey and Richard are coming over tomorrow night?'

'No, I haven't,' I said. 'Why?'

'Just wondering. You know she doesn't like red peppers, don't you?'

'Yes. Do you want me to recite the menu?'

'No, I'm sure it'll be fine.' He kissed me perfunctorily and was snoring within minutes. I lay awake next to him and tried not to think about the fact that we hadn't had sex in months. Then I went to the bathroom and lay on the bathmat for a while with a hand towel and fingers between my thighs. As I flushed the toilet later, I told myself that relationships were like economies, that they were cyclical things, with peaks and troughs. That me and Turlough were just temporarily in recession.

The dinner party was partly business and partly pleasure. 'Greasing the wheels of industry,' Turlough calls it. I feel like a fraud when I have to be nice to his clients, but he says it's essential. Everyone in Ireland seems to smell recession in the air, and Turlough's a building contractor so he needs to keep on top of things. I'm an editorial assistant at *Free Ads Weekly*—we'd never survive on my income alone.

Turlough seemed nervous that night. He looked fit, though, in his casual striped shirt and chinos—younger than his forty years.

'Have you chilled the champagne?' he asked.

'Yes,' I said, as I fastened my necklace. 'Everything's under control.'

The doorbell rang and I dabbed at my lipstick while he ran downstairs.

I heard Stacey's loud voice.

'It's fantastic to see you again, Turlough!' she said.

As I came downstairs, she was holding both of his hands, telling him how handsome he looked.

'There you are!' she exclaimed, when she saw me. 'Long time, no see!'

She kissed me once on each cheek and her perfume, like her voice, overwhelmed me. I wondered if she'd been drinking. She was dressed expensively in black and seemed flushed, excited. I felt dowdy—I'd forgotten to take my apron off.

'Where's Richard?' I asked.

'Paying the taxi,' she replied. 'Oh, here he is!'

Richard came in, shook Turlough's hand and kissed my cheek, saying, 'Lovely to see you, Melissa.'

I took the coats while Turlough led the way.

'How about a champagne cocktail?' Turlough was already swinging into his 'life and soul of the party' mode.

'Sounds fabulous, darling,' said Stacey.

'I wouldn't say no,' said Richard, spearing an olive.

At first, the evening went well. The cocktails set the pace, and I prepared an entrée of king prawns with garlic and coriander in a creamy tomato sauce while the others kept drinking. As I cleared the starters I noticed the first bottle of white wine was empty so I brought another into the dining room and handed the corkscrew to Turlough. As I did, he gave me one of those grateful glances he'd not given me for a long time, and I smiled back, before going off to check the meat. As I warmed the milk for the mash and then pummelled it, the asparagus steaming and the lamb resting, I felt more confident than I'd been in ages. Then I remembered the red wine specially chosen by Turlough. I trotted to the dining room and gave it to him. All three were chatting busily. I went back to the kitchen.

The food smelled good. I plated it like they do on *MasterChef*, a sprig of fresh rosemary on top of each pyramid of lamb, a curve of mash, a fan of green and gold vegetables, a smooth brown lake of gravy. I went back to the dining room with a plate in each hand and moved around the table to serve Stacey from her right. As she leaned towards Turlough, I had a sudden memory of working in a place called Chez Jacques twenty years previously and for a moment it felt as if they were on a date and I was their waitress.

We took a break after the main course. I cleared the plates and returned to the table with the coffee pot.

Turlough sluiced cognac into brandy glasses, then sat down

heavily. 'We brought this back from our last trip to France,' he said, as I poured coffee and splashed a little on the tablecloth.

'Oops, poor Melissa is a bit tipsy,' Stacey said, wagging her finger at me and nudging Turlough in the ribs.

'I'm not,' I said. 'I'm just a bit tired.'

'No wonder,' said Richard, and turned to me. 'Have you been following the US election at all? What do you think of McCain's running mate, that Sarah Palin?'

'I think she's dreadful,' I said.

'But she's a strong woman,' said Stacey. 'I admire strong women.'

'She's frightening, she's…' I stopped.

'She's gutsy!' exclaimed Stacey. 'I don't agree with all of her policies, of course, but she's no pushover.'

'Well, she can shoot a gun anyway,' observed Richard.

Turlough began to laugh. 'Anyone can shoot a gun,' he said. 'I'll show you. Where's my weapon, Melissa?'

'I'll get it,' I said. I left the room and came back with the gun.

'This thing is hilarious,' Turlough told them. He pushed the trigger but nothing happened.

'It needs reloading,' I said. I took out the used ring cap, replaced it with a fresh one and handed it back. Turlough aimed at the wine bottle and shot it several times. Stacey and Richard jumped in alarm, then howled with laughter.

'I want a go!' exclaimed Stacey.

'We'll all have a turn,' said Turlough, and handed it to her.

Stacey shot her husband several times and he died a mock death, writhing next to me in his chair, his head in a gunpowder halo. Then Richard took the gun. He shot Stacey once, then pulled the trigger again. This time there was no sound, just a click as the trigger fell back.

'Needs more ammo,' said Turlough.

Richard turned to me, still holding the weapon. 'Don't you want to have a go?' he asked.

'Yes,' I said. 'I have a great idea.'

I took the gun from him and used the corkscrew to dig out seven of the eight little shots from a new ring cap. Then I fitted it into the gun barrel and pressed the trigger eight times. Only one shot rang out.

'That's it,' I said. I repeated the procedure with another ring cap and pushed it into place. 'The four of us can play Russian Roulette. Just like the film.' I gave the cylinder a quick spin and clicked the gun shut.

'What film?' Stacey asked.

'*The Deer Hunter.*'

'Oh. I didn't see that.'

'Yes, you did,' said Richard. 'Robert de Niro was in it.'

'It doesn't matter,' I said. 'You'll see as we go along.'

Turlough seemed apprehensive.

'Brilliant!' said Richard. 'I'll go first.'

Bravely, he put the gun barrel to his temple. Turlough kept quiet. Stacey began to laugh.

'Stop,' said Richard. 'Don't make me laugh, you'll ruin the effect. Gosh, this feels surprisingly scary.' He pulled the trigger and nothing was heard except a click.

'Me next,' I said. I grabbed the gun, placed it to my temple as he had, and pulled the trigger. Click.

Turlough grabbed the gun dramatically and waved it like a matinee idol in an old black and white film, then shot himself in the forehead. The explosion sounded real. Everyone jumped.

'Christ,' he said. 'It *is* loud, isn't it?'

'I've not had my go,' said Stacey.

'Well,' I said. 'You're alive, aren't you? That's the whole point.' I took out the spent ring cap and prepared another round, again leaving only one live shot in place. 'Who's first this time?'

'Me,' said Richard. 'Let's go round in a clockwise direction.'

'Ok. Don't forget to give it a bit of a spin.'

Richard fired a blank.

Stacey fired a blank.

Turlough hesitated before he fired. A shot rang out.

'You're dead,' I said.

'Not again…' he moaned.

I readied the gun again, and fired a blank.

Next, Richard fired a blank.

Stacey waited and winced.

'Go on,' I said.

'Hurry up,' said Richard.

Turlough just waited, staring wide-eyed at her.

She fired. It was a blank.

Turlough fired and the shot seemed louder than before.

'I'm dead again,' he screeched. 'This is freaking me out.'

'Let's do it again,' I said.

'It's a one-in-eight chance if there are eight shots in each round, so what're the odds…?' Richard calculated in his head.

'Who wants to start?' I asked.

'Me,' said Turlough. 'I want to get it over with.' He pointed the gun at his temple this time, made a funny face, pulled the trigger. He gasped when the shot rang out. 'Fucking weird,' he said. 'We should stop this.'

'No,' said Richard. 'It's fun. Anyway, *you* can't die again, Turlough, can you? It's just not mathematically possible.'

'One more,' I said. 'There's one set of bullets left.'

'Let's go anti-clockwise this time. Me first,' said Richard. He tried several facial expressions. 'I'm imagining myself in the film,' he said. 'I'm Christopher Walken…' He contorted his face in simulated agony.

'Get a move on,' said Stacey.

'Shut up,' he said. He took a deep breath, pulled the trigger. It clicked impotently.

Before anyone could move, I took the gun, put the gun barrel in my mouth and fired. Click.

I passed it to Turlough. He fired at his forehead, a strange look on his face. Click. 'I don't believe it. I'm alive.'

Stacey was next. 'I don't think I like this game any more,' she said. She shut her eyes and squeezed the trigger. The shot was so loud I expected blood, and the bullet left a smoky aura round her head. She sat there, holding the gun, not saying a word.

'You're dead, Stacey,' said Richard. 'And it's time to go home.'

I stood at the door and waved goodbye as the rear lights of the taxi vanished into the night.

'Well, that's the last we'll see of her,' I said. 'She's history.'

'What do you mean?' said Turlough.

'You know what I mean.'

'For Christ's sake,' he said. 'I don't know what you're getting at.' I felt beaten.

'And anyway…' he added.

'I know what you're going to say. I forgot the dessert.'

'To hell with the dessert.' He swallowed the last of his brandy and put the glass down. Then he came towards me and began to grope me like he hadn't done in years. We didn't even reach our bed—half-torn clothes on the carpet, sucking and fucking like mad things.

He didn't roll away afterwards. He just lay there on top of me. Only his chest heaved, as he cried quietly. I lay underneath him, my arms outstretched. I couldn't seem to raise them, not even to comfort him.

I've taken the gun out of the junk drawer and looked at it several times since then. I know I should throw it out, but I can't seem to let it go.

STAG

LUKE WOODS

The escalator that brings you up to street-level—its angle of ascent, its rapid tempo, its seeming endlessness—makes you want to knock one of the other boys down, and watch the giant moving staircase abort his fall. Picture it: the slow tumble of Gobbie's round body like a shirt in a dryer, tumble flip, tumble curse. Juggled by a machine. Before you can share the joke, the ride is over. Swing eyes across a virgin cityscape, form a first impression of Prague. Elder Bugger starts up a club chant, and soon the entire stag-party is bouncing the four words off of pastry cake buildings and into the early night sky.

> *Oh your wife eats testicles,*
> *Your wife eats testicles,*
> *Your wife eats testicles,*
> *Your wife eats testicles.*

It's cold out tonight. January. Obligatory. Stick hands into pockets, open the stiff denim with wriggled fingers (your pants are tight, it shows you care). There is no warmth to be found in the sleeves that receive you. Think of the clothes you packed for the weekend—there isn't a single warm scrap, not even a little cotton condom of a hat to cover your pink and glowing ears. Whatever. Drink it off, you think, drink off this fucking air. The hostel is only a few blocks away (well done Gobbie, well planned) and the long room with twelve bunk beds continues the pattern of narrow spaces you've shared with your friends today: Tube to plane, plane to bus, bus to Tube to chute-shaped room. And soon shoes are kicked off, and there is a queue for the shitter and turns are waited to shave and splash water on faces and rub deodorant over armpits and jerk semen out of over-eager and anticipatory pricks; all the usual pre-party run-around. And by the time you reach the bathroom the floor is wet, and towels are flung to one corner and the mirror is steamed and smudged with palm prints. Wipe a swathe of reflection and take a look. Hello. Slap the paste from your cheeks; draw a basin of tepid water. Lather your thick neck, the stubble of a day's travel. Scrape of a safety razor, yellow piss in the toilet bowl. From under the soapbeard fresh skin emerges. Press a hot towel against it, pores open and blood lets from the two inevitable nicks that have plagued you since you first started shaving. Through the white wooden door you can hear the excitement growing, the high-crowed 'Tossers' which trump the other insults in jest and decibel. Pout into the mirror, draw your mouth into the cold hard line of a man who is not to be fucked with. A man who is sexy, mysterious, English. Squint your eyes and practise letting the countenance slowly crack, curling your mouth into a cool, satisfied smile. Nice. Natural. Product and aftershave finish the dance. Zip your fly and let the next man in.

And after the greedy pizza slurps and a dozen or so pitchers of beer (when a man eats, he eats on autopilot, and when a group of men eat, nothing is said or thought, and nothing is noteworthy, and no sensation is new) the night begins. The stag takes a left turn into a small cocktail lounge. Pointing at the menu, a few mangled attempts to wrangle unfamiliar Slavic consonants. The bar girl smiles as she brings the drinks over, and her round tits strain against a tight cotton T-shirt, but before you allow your countenance to crack open (naturally) she is turned away and bobbing her shoulders to whatever island mush is the rage these days. You never did like those Caribbean rhythms. Too skittery. Never know which beat to bob your head on. It's as if they existed explicitly to discourage Englishmen from dancing. The vernacular syncopations have none of the democratic edge of house music, where the quarter note lords supreme, and every element orbits the One, and every body falls into step automatically. The head jerk, fist pump and crotch thrust all timed and running like pistons. A dance machine. You can be a dance machine. Look at the pool of blue set down in front of you, the ice cubes bobbing in brilliant turquoise. Draw the hue up through a black straw and swallow. Sweet gin based something. Gone, gone, gone. And, as you wait for the bar girl to make her way back over, The Bugger Boys discover something worthwhile. A bucket. The Bugger Boys talk at once, as one, and in their four-hand motion you understand. The tits will make you a bucket of booze. A ten-in-one is what the sign says, and in a couple of heartbeats the order is placed. You wait, watching as the glacier, the forest, and the distillery find their way into the large clear container. You watch toned forearms ripple as she stirs sugar sludge up from the bottom, you watch as her shirt lifts up to expose a bit of back tattoo when she reaches high above her head to pull down a handful of large pink straws, as she plants them like flags in amongst the ice field with a calculating and mock serious frown. Bucket served to The Bugger Boys, and all at once the entire stag crew is ordering big drinks in groups. Four men to a ten drink. Two if you're burly. Zombies and Mojitos. Elder Bugger wants a Sex on the Beach, who will share with him? You know the answer already.

You are standing on the corner of some square. Well-lit. Buzzing. The limits of specificity have been reached. What the fuck did that bartender give you? It was the color of antifreeze, big wedge of pineapple sticking out of the glass. Ahead you see the man of the hour, Peanut, sweet doomed Peanut, leading the charge down a bright side alley. Large lettered signs pop off of buildings and communicate neon-big words. *Cabaret, Ladies, Exotic.* Exotic. That sounds nice. Gobbie calls out to you, the group, the street—'Wanna get a quick sausage, you know, 'fore slipping one yourself?' Forward motion stalls at the suggestion of meat, and soon the whole stag is following Gobbie's lead. 'Tits! You can buy a shot on the street. Civilisation. We've found her at last. Who wants one?' Swarm with the rest of the boys around the kiosk; straddle the feet of some greasy ground-locked beggar. His mangy dog looks up at you and grins. Gobbie is gesturing at rows of sausage excitedly, his English comes out slow and loud. He slows down as he drinks. Turns to sludge. The beggar has struggled off the pavement, he is kneeling at cock-level saying something Czech. The language sounds like someone sneezing kernels of corn. Shake your head no. He starts to gesture, an index finger stabs a filthy palm.

'Listen mate, I don't speak Czech.' Good. Nice and slow, understandable.

More index finger stabbing. More snot corn.

'I. Don't. Speak. Czech.' Better. Firm. Turn your back. Pretend the beggar isn't there, only inches away from the crack of your ass.

Looking at the backlit menu board your eyes unglue the information contained within each glowing sausage; involuntarily they gloss over the mess of jumbled letters polluting the bottom of each picture. Number eleven looks good, yeah, number eleven. Mustard, onions, watered-down ketchup.

Gobbie sends a small paper cup around the left side of your head.

'Here's a little one then, drink up.'

Vodka, greasy and clear. Its liquid fingers fan out through the soup your stomach is simmering, the glossy booze sinks quick to the bottom of your gut.

'Man up, round two.'

Raise the paper cup, drink, breathe through your nose. The fruity taste of the cocktail has disappeared.

The sausage bird is waiting for your order, but you're too busy thinking of vodka's uncluttered descent to notice until she starts saying 'Yes?' repeatedly. Scramble—number eleven—say it loud.

'Beer, baby?'

Before you can nod she has already turned her back, opened the icebox and pulled out a can of Gambrinus. You watch in awe as she manoeuvres the tube of hotcrisp pig with her long acrylic nails, throws it down on the paper tray and pumps a puddle of mustard from the dispenser. A single, articulated motion.

'Seventy-five, baby.' Look at her face for the first time. She is not unattractive — a standard service-industry slut — good for a go in the park. Smile a crooked smile, puff out your chest. Pull out your wallet and reach inside: a lone 2000 crown note. Wave the big bill, half apologetically and half like it makes you more desirable.

'That's big money, baby. That all you have?' Her eyes flash past you to the queue behind. You nod and she sighs and gives you the just-a-moment sign and ducks below the counter. Around you people order from the secondary sausage bird and wave money over your head. It's better not to move. Let them stream around you. Decide upon the best way to eat the sausage, then break a little chunk off the end and dip it in mustard. Pop the meat into your mouth and recoil at the heat, the steam that releases when the casing is punctured. Swallow and feel the sausage drop, its solid hot tumble so different from the vodka's quick slip. Tear a piece of bread and fold it onto your tongue. Peer over the griddle into the kiosk, but your eyes can't take the meat smoke and the heat. Blink, take another bite of your pig. Where did your change go? Crack the beer's sealed silver cylinder and take a healthy swallow. Let the liquid pump your Adam's apple. God, how you love to consume. Look at your bread. Eat it. From below the deck of the good ship Sausage your bird reappears. In her hand the candy coloured bank notes of the Czech Republic. It is a mountain of change, and she hands it over sourly, counting off each 200-crown note with a soft foreign number, stopping when you're square. Trust the math and wad the notes into your wallet, wad the wallet into the back left pocket of your acid-abused and artfully ripped jeans. Collect your consumables from the counter of the kiosk, turn towards the stag party. Not there. Fuck, fuck, fuck are your thoughts. Look around this bright square, perk your ears and listen for a loud battle-hymn bouncing off of plastered walls, off-key and exuberant. Nobody. No Gobbie or Mr Skelator, no Bugger Boys. The eleven pale friends you arrived with and the matching black polo shirts they are wearing have disappeared into the night.

Decide that drunks flow downhill and pick the widest avenue. Focus on the glowing cabaret signs and chart a course. Pile the rest of the sausage into your mouth, start baptising the meat with beer before it has been swallowed. Ease back the pig/hop porridge. Drop the can and paper plate on the ground and start walking. On your way past the beggar, your left hand reaches out involuntarily to drop some coin on the coin rag below.

Look at your watch—watch those digital numbers and their double swim spin. Squint them into submission. 12:56. You're right on time to see the skeleton on the astrological clock animate and toll the tiny bell, but the line you cut through Old Town Square is a drunken diagonal that leads away from the mechanical saint parade.

From across the square you've been spotted stumbling. Unseen lips and eyes roll up in a tight, satisfied smile. The man you run into makes it seem providence has crossed your paths. A happy accident. You hear him call out; the pitch a high tenor and the accent North African.

'Hey, my friend, you want to go to cabaret.' It is a statement.

Turn to look him in his four big white pupils. Squint. Bring the pictures back together, stop the left eye's lazy drift. He's smiling at you and talking. You're nodding. Tune back in.

'… Five free pints…'

That is enough for any man, but his words have already triggered another image, one of neon signs floating in a black void. *Cabaret, Exotic, Girls, Girls, Girls.*

'… Beautiful girls man, any one you want. C'mon, I'll take you. Pussy Palace.'

'Pussy Palace?'

'Pussy Palace.'

It certainly sounds like somewhere the stag party had planned to end up; some place with the word 'Pussy' blazing red. Nod at the hustler; follow his slow shuffle across the square. Pick a building to focus on. Bring the images back together—close the eye that lies and watch the ghost structure vanish. Close your other eye and trip over an upthrust cobblestone. Skin your knee, mash dirt and pigeon shit into fresh blood and flesh. The hustler watches as you use your right arm as a tripod, your slow evolution to bipedal motion. Head heavy. Mouth dry. Finger the factory issued rip in the knee of your jeans. Dust off your polo shirt, pop its collar and renew your sense of purpose. Under his breath, the hustler whistles a simple legato melody. An endless two-bar loop. He takes a sharp left out of Old Town Square and down a winding side street. Brace against a champagne coloured Alpha Romeo station wagon. Your guide is patient; he waits as you double over, as you attempt to shake the weight from between your ears. He walks slowly, makes sure you see when he takes a left, makes sure you know what alleyway he is stepping into. The buildings in this city all look the same, the same stone foundations bowed with time. Pause and look down an unlit street: an indecipherable dappling of black. From the shadows you hear your guide urge you on.

'Not much farther, my man, not much farther.'

The soft sodium illumination of Old Town has vanished. Your guide cannot see you, but still he knows exactly where you are.

Stop in front of an unmarked metal door. The hustler smiles wide again, but the inflection is different this time and, based on your knowledge of strip-clubs, what lies behind this thick black door is either non-existent or stuffed with unspeakable riches. The hustler sticks out both palms and says 'My friend, this is where you give me my money.' Instinctively you reach for your ass, extract your wallet. Press a wad of uncounted green and orange currency into his hands. It might as well be confetti. The Pussy Palace smile returns. He knocks on the door. A small rectangle slides open, and a pair of eyes inspect you. Slowly the door swings into the night, and you hear a reassuring pump—the robotic drum majors and synthetic fireworks of a techno parade. The rectangle of black light spilling into the street is your personal purple carpet, and with a drunken, delicate foot you step up into the building. Ahead of you stands a man with an improbable moustache, an imposing and twirled hazelnut rope. He wears a black tuxedo with a red cravat. A vein pulses across the shining expanse of his forehead.

'Welcome, my friend. Welcome to the Pussy Palace.' He leads you through a set of red-velvet curtains—catchers of disease, mufflers of sound. Your body slips through the soft-red flaps. You're led through a vaulted and unadorned concrete corridor to the entrance of the club. As you step through the doorway, the circle of sight dissolves and full vision is granted. Your eyes flood. A long catwalk laid through the room. A raised and lacquered wooden tongue studded with taste buds diffusing an incidental glow. Around the tongue a ring of low-backed vinyl couches. On one a smoky yellow mountain slouches with his shirt half-buttoned and pipe bulge in his white khakis. A bar runs the length of the far wall. No sign of The Bugger Boys or Peanut or Gobbie The show hasn't started, and you want nothing to drink. Focus on the music instead.

All it takes is a slow filter-pan from the DJ and the music, and the room encased inside the music, modulates. The sugar sound that spills from the speakers suggests that time is slowing down to accommodate you and you feel your heart beat for what seems to be the first time in ages. You can be a dance machine.

The beat propels you to an unoccupied couch near the front of the tongue. The music swells as frequencies are reintroduced to the mix, and the men around you clap in anticipation. Slap those hands together. Reiterate the only beat. Gaze up the catwalk as the first legs appear—greased and slender in high red stockings that connect with straps to a see-though lacy topthing where silicon factories chug. She is blonde in yellow light and stepping off the tongue into the crowd, she is followed and the One comes again—Beat. Beat. Beat. And the music is filter-swept and the lights burn auburn over tan skin and chestnut hair. And your neck snaps down on a rest

—and your eyes drop accordingly and fall on a pair of truncated legs; small turned branches supporting a delicate fetal form dressed in supple and matured flesh, ever so slightly fat. From her lowered vantage point the midget makes eye contact with you. Nod to the beat. Your eyes lock and as the midget rounds the tongue's parabolic axis she swings a small ass-cheek your way in a glitchy and poly-rhythmic display of muscle control. She is diminishing into shadows before you notice the next One, and the room shades red and her skin is young southern fruit and her hair an electric blood orange. Ass. Twitch. Ass. Twitch. Forms that shrink to firm head beats. And the stripper belt continues to churn on stage, and onto the club floor girls gear forward. And two small eyes look up, and lock again, and one small hand with child fingers rubs gentle thigh circles.

Look easy over short times, and your mind returns to the One, and you feel a strange hip twist, and knotted in stuttering beats your crotch and body are pulled into this mazurka, this frantic twitch brought on by gnome proportions, tiny globular breasts and a pigeon ribcage. And small finger circles expand, they orbit around your crotch, they take a slow walk up stained and dirty trousers. Lean back onto the couch, and the room filters into a deep violet, and time slows down to a point where there is only the One, infinitely sub-divisible and nuanced. And your little guide crawls forward for the rest of the night, her head slung low between two miniscule shoulders, her small hands outstretched.

Welcome to the Pussy Palace, my friend.

Tonight you take the midget.

THE BOYS

EMILY FIRETOG

Rich flew home from Berlin on Monday night and called Dad from the airport. He was in America for the first time in two years. Dad, who hadn't gotten in his car in the past three months after having a minor fender bender with a parked truck, drove to the airport to pick him up. Rich was talking a lot and fast, and Dad wasn't sure if he was on drugs or just not on his medication. At home, they talked until the middle of the night and then went to bed. When Dad woke up, he said he already knew—that there was a feeling in the house. He walked down to the kitchen, saw the basement door was open, and went down the stairs. Rich had slit his wrists. He was cold. There was blood on the floor, but not as much, Dad said, as he thought there would have been.

I had told Gary to stay home.

'James, are you sure? You don't want me to come with you?' he said.

'I need to go by myself first. I'll call you when I get there.'

'I want to be there for you. For you *and* your dad.'

Those little lies you tell to keep your relationship stable don't matter when your brother's just killed himself. I didn't reassure Gary that he was there for us—I didn't tell him anything at all.

On the train to Newport everyone was asleep. Even though all the lights were off I couldn't see anything out the window. I looked at the reflection of the inside of the car, the mirroring of my head against the window, the small fog my breath made against the glass. I couldn't sleep. I had taken three days off from work. Rich would still be dead when I got back. Dad might even be dead. You can never know when things will happen.

I thought about the phone call from Dad. I tried to remember it word for word but mostly what stuck with me was this horrible choking sound he made. I'd never heard him make that sound before. I had never heard anyone make that sound.

'Dad, you there?'

'That's it,' he said after a minute. 'He did it. He's dead.'

He made the sound again. It was horrible.

'Okay, Dad, okay. I'll be on a train in a couple hours. I'll be in by the morning,' I said.

'That's good, that's good,' he paused. 'Just you?'

'Just me, Dad.'

The cab driver dropped me off in front of the house and I walked straight to the back yard. I figured if Dad was still sleeping I shouldn't wake him. I sat on one of the lawn chairs on the porch and took a pack of cigarettes out of my bag. There was so much silence. I'd forgotten what the suburbs could feel like—that terrifying stillness. The grass was overgrown and the roof of the shed, where the shingles looked rotten, had fallen in on one side. I promised myself I would mow the lawn while I was there. I could call someone to fix the shed too. I sat smoking cigarettes for a while. The sun moved up over the fence and warmed the air. I left a message for Gary at work telling him I got there okay. He called me back right away.

'I was on a conference call. If you left a message longer than thirty seconds I would have been able to pick up.'

'Sorry.'

'How's your dad?' he said.

'I haven't seen him yet.'

'Where are you?'

'In the back yard.'

'James, go inside and see your father.'

'I will,' I said.

'I couldn't fall asleep last night, I was thinking about you. Did you sleep on the train?'

'Not really.'

'I miss you.'

'Me too.'

'Okay, go find your dad.'

'Right. I'll call you later.'

'I love you.'

'Love you, too.'

I heard the screen door opening behind me and rubbed my cigarette into the arm of the chair.

'So you're smoking again?' Dad said.

'Want?'

'Maybe later. Don't leave it there, no one's going to clean up after you here.'

I put the hot cigarette butt in my pocket and followed him inside. We sat down on the couch in the living room.

'Have you been up long? I didn't want to wake you.'

'I know. I saw the taxi pull up. I couldn't sleep. Thought I'd give you some time though.'

'Thanks.'

He put his hand on my knee for a moment, then brought it back to his lap.

We sank back into the couch. I was about to ask if he had eaten anything but he had started crying, his hands over his face. Then that terrible sound came out of him. His shoulders spasmed. I put my arms around him—not exactly hugging him but holding him down against the couch, applying pressure. I tried to see where the telephone was.

'What could I do?' he said softly.

'Nothing,' I said.

He wiped his eyes with the heels of his hands and then leaned back. He tapped me on the knee a few times and took deep breaths. I looked at his hands, old hands full of wrinkles, liver spots, blue veins.

'Rich was sick,' I said.

When my mother died, Rich was still living at home and Dad was regulating his medication. He hadn't had an episode in six months; he wasn't working much but seemed okay. The wake was at my mom's sister's house. When we got home, we sat around the living room while Gary made sandwiches for us in the kitchen. Rich had started shaving his head completely bald, and it was then, sitting in the living room that night, that I noticed a striking resemblance between Rich and my father. They could have been holy men of the same order.

We were watching an awards show. Mom must have set the television to record it because the channel turned from the news to the awards show in the middle of the weather report. None of us got up to change it.

'It's like Mom's back from the grave,' Rich said. He was trying to joke around.

'Not now,' I said.

'We're all sad, Richard. Don't be stupid,' Dad said.

'I can't feel anything with all this shit I'm on,' he said, stuttering on the word shit.

'You don't feel sad that Mom died?' I asked.

'I know she died. I feel bad, I know I'm sad. But I don't feel it. I can't feel anything!'

'You know what then,' Dad started—he started and should have stopped but didn't—'then stop taking the fucking medication. I don't care.'

'I'm going to hold you to that,' Rich said getting up. He pointed his finger at Dad like a gameshow host and smiled with the left side of his face. We heard him go to his bedroom and shut the door.

'You shouldn't have said that, Dad,' I said.

'I mean, what kind of pills are they that he can't cry when his mother dies?'

'He needs those. He needs to take his pills.'

'I don't need you telling me how to raise my son.'

Then Gary walked in with his plate of triangle sandwiches, which was about the worst time in the world he could have.

He put them down at the card table behind where I was sitting. I could feel him looking at Dad and I could see Dad looking at him. It was only the second or third time they had met, though I had been with Gary for almost six years. They would never get along, no matter how hard Gary tried. Gary nodded and smiled like an abused child foolishly waiting for the last slap.

'You want to tell me how to raise Richard too?' Dad said, standing up and turning off the television.

'Sorry?' Gary said.

'Look what you've left me with, Helen!' Dad said, raising his hands.

'Are you looking for an Oscar, Dad?' I said.

'Why couldn't I have a normal life? Why am I left here with you? You know we made a deal, Mom and I—I was going to go first.'

'Sorry we're not what you expected.'

He sighed. 'James, everything isn't about you. I'm just saying—'

'No, Dad, you're right: a faggot and a schizophrenic? You really pulled the short straw with us.'

'James,' Gary said.

'James,' Dad said.

'What? Let's go, Gary, I can mourn at home.'

'James, I'm sorry, don't go.' Dad put the palms of his hands together: a prayer.

But I left. I made Gary go to the car without saying goodbye to anyone. On my way out I stuck my head into Rich's bedroom.

'Rich, we're heading home.'

He was on his bed looking up at the ceiling.

'I'm going to go to Europe and do some travelling,' he said without getting up.

'Why do you want to do that?'

'There's a girl I met at Dicey's that's doing something over there and I want to go stay with her,' he said.

'We can talk about this later, Rich. I have to go.'

'Okay,' he said.

Rich had brought his laptop home with him. Dad asked me to go through it and see if there was anything on it. What he really wanted to know was if there was a note. I tried to turn on the computer but it wouldn't light up.

'Maybe the battery died,' Dad said.

I turned it over. I didn't know what I was looking for, I didn't know too much about computers. Then I realised there was no hard drive—he must have taken it out. Some paranoid thing. I was relieved he had taken it.

'Do you think we can find it?' Dad asked.

'I don't think so.'

'It's okay,' he said.

'Do you want to go have a cigarette with me?'

'Yes,' he said.

We went outside to the back porch and sat on the deck chairs. I rubbed the black spot where I put my cigarette out earlier. I handed a cigarette to Dad and gave him my lighter. He clicked the lighter twice but he couldn't get the flame up. He handed the cigarette back to me.

'Can't light it on the third try,' he said, 'bad luck.'

I lit both cigarettes and handed one back to him. He took a deep breath and let the smoke come out of his nose so that his head was slowly surrounded by a thin grey cloud.

'Where's Rich?' I asked.

He coughed. 'His body?'

I nodded.

'The ambulance took it to the morgue. We have to call them today and tell them what to do with the body. I'm not sure, really. I know what Mom would have wanted…'

'I'll take care of it,' I said.

He took a business card out of his pocket and gave it to me with a shaky hand. I took it and put it in my wallet.

'What about the blood?' I asked. I figured: get it all out now, just one swoop.

'They'll send someone to take care of it. They should be here this afternoon.'

'A cleaner?'

'For blood,' he said.

'What a job.'

'I can't even imagine.'

We were silent for a while.

'What do you think of taking the boat out?' Dad asked suddenly.

'Today?' I looked at my watch. It was only ten o'clock.

'I haven't been out in a couple months. You probably haven't been out in years.'

'At least.'

'I could use the help,' he said.

'I'd like to. I didn't bring the right shoes though.'

Dad shot me a look.

'I can look around, I'm sure there's something,' I said.

I let Dad finish his cigarette and put mine out, putting the butt in my pocket again. I went into Rich's bedroom where all my old things were stored. In the closet our clothes were mixed together. I crouched down and looked for a pair of shoes I could wear. I pulled a wool sweater off a hanger. I didn't know if it was Rich's or mine.

Rich's first break was when he was fifteen, and after that he wasn't as much my brother as a person who inhabited my brother's body. I was eight. I didn't know what had happened, but I saw that a fuse had blown in him and he was swallowed, gone. Only my mother saw her son in him anymore; my father and I learned to live around him, circling him so we rarely ever touched.

A month after the funeral Rich went to live with a girl in Berlin. When she kicked him out he moved to a shelter for a little while, and then a squat. I had gone to see him once. I asked him to come home but he said he liked where he was; he said he was happy. I don't think I had ever heard him say he was happy before. I asked him to go to the free-clinic pharmacy; we went together and got prescriptions filled. He said he would start taking them again and that he wanted to get better. I bought him new shoes and sweaters, a couple bags of groceries. I don't know if I believed him, but I said I did and went back to America.

I drove Dad's car to the dock by the A Lot where all the Class 1 ships were. Some of the fishermen who had pulled in a good load were already coming in. Dad used to be one of them. He used to come home smelling of fish blood—a sour smell, like thick seawater. He would change in the bathroom by the garage and hand his clothes to Mom in a green garbage bag so he wouldn't smell up the rest of the house. He would show Rich and me where the line had caught his hand that day and the gash he had because of it.

'No big deal,' he would say. 'All in a day's work.'

The boat was named Helen, after Mom. Dad paid a kid that was running around the dock ten dollars to unwrap the tarp from the sails and deck. We got on and Dad mechanically unwound the sails. He was slow but unthinking; he touched a rope and then a lever and they moved the way they were meant to. His old body looked alive, he stood up straighter and stretched out his arms and took a deep breath. He extended on the boat, he became huge. I sat down on the bench off the starboard and watched him.

'You know the rods and lines are below deck, we could try and fish if you're up for it,' Dad said.

'Okay,' I said, getting up, 'what else should I get?'

'Just bring up two rods and the bait box.'

I went down through the floor and passed up the rods and the red toolbox where Dad kept the neon fishing bait. It was the same as always.

Dad hooked up the rods and looked through the box.

'Where's the knife?' He looked up at me and his face creased around his eyes as if he were squinting at the sun.

'I don't know, Dad.'

'There's supposed to be one in here,' he said. He looked for it. He went into the drawers under the seats. There was a secret door near the steering wheel and he looked there too. He couldn't find it.

'Maybe it's at home,' I said.

'I don't take it home.'

'Maybe it fell overboard?'

'You think that's what happened to it, James, you really think?'

'I don't know, Dad.'

'Maybe. Maybe it fell overboard,' he said, sitting down next to me.

'Do you want me to go to the Local and get one? I'm sure they sell something there.'

'No,' he said. 'No, it's fine.'

'Do you want to head out?'

'I don't know.'

'Okay, Dad, let's sit,' I said. 'Let's just sit for a while.'

THE FIRST TIME
SHIH-LI KOW

'You're late,' Mimi says but it is without annoyance. She has known Mei Kwan for far too long to be upset by these things. 'Hurry up, third room. He's waited ten minutes.'

'Who?' Mei Kwan kicks her shoes under the rack by the door.

'That bald doctor who likes you.'

Mei Kwan unfastens the top two buttons of her shirt. There is no time for make-up. The doctor prefers the lights off anyway. She pushes open the door of the third room.

She remembered the first time she met Ah Wai. He was waiting outside the school gates for his younger sister, her classmate. Sixteen and thin with no distinctive features except for purple streaks in his hair, he looked ill at ease in the swarm of students with school regulation crew cuts. He was so proud of his tattoo, the Chinese character for 'Death' inked in black on his forearm, and not so proud that he had stopped schooling.

The man grunts his fleeting pleasure. Mei Kwan lets him lie atop her for a few breaths before reaching for the digital clock on the bedside shelf. Glowing red, the numbers have marked his time. She rolls his bulk off her.

The first time Ah Wai held her hand was on that day that his sister skipped school. He came anyway to walk Mei Kwan home. In a show of nonchalance, they had strolled, looking in opposite directions. In the midday heat, her hand felt the dampness start in his palm. Too conscious of the feel of skin, they walked in silence. The friendly, comfortable chatter that accompanied their usual journeys home fell by the wayside for the day.

Mimi lets someone else into the room. Mei Kwan does not notice his appearance, only that he is in a hurry and averts his eyes from hers. He stares at a spot on the wall above her pillow and rushes. Rocks and rushes until he is spent.

The first time they kissed was at a bus stop. They had tried in vain to outrun the rain chasing them to the shelter. No hands, just Ah Wai's lips, first against her damp cheek, then on her mouth. A kiss like a long drink of water. The taste of clean rain. The memory of water falling like a sheet all around, slippers and trouser legs soaked from splashing across puddles.

'You're actually quite pretty,' says the next man, his tongue against the side of her neck. She turns her face away. Windows do not exist in the third room.

'Of course,' she replies in a rehearsed banter. 'Come and see me again tomorrow. I'll be even prettier.'

'Ah Kwan, come out and have a drink. Ah Wai brought us tea and dumplings,' Mimi calls through the door.

'Has he gone back downstairs already?'

'Yes. Looks like a busy night.' They sit at the Formica-topped table by the window. Mei Kwan lifts the curtain and peers through the slot where a glass pane has broken. She sees Loke Fatt Restaurant across the road. The stove fire flares high and makes whooshing sounds. Ah Wai is shaking a big wok with one hand, his other hand tirelessly pushes ingredients around with an oversized ladle. His left arm, the one with the tattoo, is larger than his right from nights of lifting the heavy cast-iron wok. An arm named 'Death' cooking up plate after plate of steaming noodles.

'Good. We could use the money. My older boy is starting school next year,' Mei Kwan says.

'Oh, Ling Ling is quitting next month. Getting married,' Mimi says, breaking open a dumpling to reveal the lotus paste centre. She offers Mei Kwan one half.

'To that *fei chai*, the plump boy who used to come here? The one with the father who owns a hardware shop?'

Mimi nods, her mouth full. She grins and sticks out a fist with her thumb up. Way to go, Ling Ling.

The second time they tried to get married was when Ah Wai was offered the only job he ever had that came with an employment letter. Night security guard at a Japanese glove factory. It came with three sets of uniforms and a small salary large enough for them to rent a room without an attached bath. Ah Wai's parents would not hear of it.

'Go put some make up on,' Mimi says. 'You're looking tired.'

'I am. The baby doesn't sleep in the day. That means I can't get any rest.'

Ah Wai's parents saw her for the first time on the second day of a Chinese New Year so long ago she could not remember the year. His mother did not like her blue, glittery eyeshadow. Mei Kwan could read her disapproval in the way she set her drink on the table, as if she did not care if the drink spilled or the glass broke. Ah Wai's father talked only to his son and ignored her.

The next man smells of sweat, cigarette smoke, garlic and beer. He grips her hair too hard. She winces but the pain is bearable, not enough to let a cry out. Be a good sport, otherwise they won't come back, Mimi had said that so many years ago.

The first time they made love was in his house, emptied of his family who had gone on a beach holiday. In his bed on a cotton sheet printed with maple leaves. She was seventeen and cried tears of confusion after. Ah Wai dressed her carefully and held her close. For the first time, he said what he would often say for years to come, 'I will take care of you.'

Sounds of mirth come from the next room. Coco's trilling laugh and a man's rumble. Coco could always laugh. Until she stopped marvelling at the generosity of Coco's humour, Mei Kwan found it unbelievable that her co-worker's laughter could be shared with the men. Mei Kwan's is reserved for Mimi and the girls only. Coco is not pretty but she could laugh as if she meant it.

His first present to her was a teddy bear holding a heart-shaped cushion the size of an apple. It was a keepsake from a day at the travelling fair that came to town during the school holidays. How she had laughed at his fear of heights, high up on the ferris wheel, swaying at the apex in a gondola that looked like a wire basket and the world below an eternity away.

'I wish my wife were more like you,' the man says. He flicks his cigarette and ashes sprinkle the floor. Mei Kwan feels a prickle of annoyance but she says, 'Ai, a wife cannot be the same. How can you eat abalone every day, ya or not? Sometimes, you must eat chicken.' It is a stale joke but he chuckles.

The bed creaks when he gets up. She puts her hand out to take the twenty ringgit he offers. 'Tip for you, don't need to tell Mimi.'

'Come after work tomorrow. Try some sharksfin. I'll make you feel eighteen again.'

The first night she went to work for Mimi, Ah Wai drank himself to the brink of violence. He drove his fist into the bedroom door and punched a splinter-edged hole that clawed his hand. He disappeared for three days and came home when protective scabs had formed over the wounds on his hand. Sober and subdued, he started work at Loke Fatt Restaurant to be near her. Washing dishes, scrubbing and scrubbing away at the stubborn grease that clung to the plastic plates, keeping his eyes away from the curtained window across the road. Water ran continuously from the washing tap by the pavement.

It is 5.45 a.m. The night is over. Mei Kwan washes her face at the bathroom sink. The cheap mascara is hard to remove. She rubs her eyelids with a cotton pad soaked in baby oil.

When the midwife put Mei Kwan's newborn baby on her chest, she remembered nothing but the feel of a tiny, downy head against her chin. The first time she saw Ah Wai cradling their unblemished baby, she wanted him to scrape off that word tattooed on his arm. She wanted that and so much more but she smiled back at him.

Ah Wai comes through the doors stretching his neck from side to side, flexing his tired shoulders. Mimi yawns. 'Ah Kwan, your bodyguard is here. Better go home and get some sleep.'

'OK, I'll get going. If the baby sleeps, maybe I'll boil a pot of green bean soup for tomorrow. See you.'

They step out from the stairwell into a pool of orange light from the tungsten street lamp overhead.

'Wait, let me go light a joss stick,' Mei Kwan turns into the small temple next to Mimi's place. The temple is still dark but its doors are never locked. The air is clean, the swirling smoke that fills its insides during the day has dissipated in the night. Ah Wai lights her joss sticks with his lighter. She raises them to her forehead between her palms. Garbed in stainless white porcelain, the Goddess of Mercy looks down from her pedestal with a benevolent smile barely discernible in the darkness.

Thank you, Mei Kwan says silently. She stabs the three joss sticks into a big urn of ashes and smoke curls upwards from the burning tips.

Ah Wai takes her hand in his and starts talking about going fishing that evening. Back out on the street, he looks at her and today, misses the sneers of the schoolboys at the bus stop who turn to look at them. Boys Ah Wai's age fifteen years ago see a woman with yellow hair, tattooed eyebrows turning a blue tinge and too short a skirt. They see the years showing around her mouth and the corners of her eyes. Their eyes ridicule a man in a faded shirt, with dirty fingernails and greasy, grey streaked hair growing too long over his ears. Their own uniforms are white and crisply starched in the early morning, their brows not yet furrowed.

Mei Kwan feels a familiar little knot with feathery tentacles play in the pit of her stomach. She recognises it as the periphery of fear.

'Ah Wai, there aren't enough days...' she falters.

'... in this life?' he offers quietly.

'Yes.' Days of absolute certainty not clouded by shadows of men cast by red light bulbs, sniggers of puberty-fresh schoolboys and the drudgery of an imperfect life. Days when what is gained has more reality and colour than that lost.

The sky starts to lighten. Signs of life and the clatter of roller shutters being raised awaken the sleeping shops. Ah Wai rubs the small of her back. She rests her head lightly on his shoulder, falling into step with him. She inhales the familiar scent of stale cooking oil on him and cool morning air. He has a smile on his face. The schoolboys look away as Mei Kwan climbs behind Ah Wai on the motorbike and locks her arms around his waist.

A LOT YOU DON'T KNOW

JAMES MOYNIHAN

Wisdom—like wealth—is not evenly distributed on the planet. I am an independent financial advisor—in other words people pay me to tell them what to do with their money. My wife, Fiona, is a gynaecologist. We live in County Kildare, thirty miles from Dublin. We work hard.

We have two daughters. Maebh will finish secondary school this year. She's top of her class in most subjects. She plays hockey and paints in her spare time. Our second girl, Francesca, is thirteen years old. She's just started second year. Francesca is not as academically inclined as Maebh. She's different.

A few years ago my mother died. When we got home after the burial Maebh hung up her coat and started reciting the periodic table of elements around the house. My wife was coaching her.

'What do you call the Group 8 or Group O elements?'

'The Noble gases!'

'Why?'

'Because their outer shells are full and they don't need any electrons and they don't want to donate any!'

'Correct! What is the first alkali metal in the table?'

'Hydrogen-Helium-Lithium… Lithium?'

'Why are they called alkali metals?'

'Because they form hydroxides…'

I went to the front door and got outside. I looked up at the grey sky and felt myself drawn away to go for a walk. I didn't know where I was going. I drifted down towards the traffic lights until I heard fast footsteps behind me. Francesca caught up with me and I stopped.

'How far we going, Dad?'

I said,

'A long way, Fran, long walkabout.'

She walked along with me for a while and then said, 'Walking is good, sometimes.'

She caught me up exactly right. She just walked beside me—no more words—just walking until we got tired, and the two of us went home again.

But anyway, that was three years ago, when she was ten.

About two weeks ago I got home from work late, drove into the driveway and pressed the remote control button above my head in the car. The garage door opened and I drove my eleven-year-old BMW into the garage, switched off the engine and pressed the button on the remote controller again. The garage door closed down behind the car. I wanted to breathe there for a minute or two before going into the house.

As I sat there, I heard the front door of the house slam. I got out of the car and went into the kitchen. I walked along the hall and called up the stairs, 'Maebh, Francesca, are you here?'

Maebh came out of her room, stood at the top of the stairs and said, 'Yeah, Dad.'

She sort of slid her arm down the banister and asked, 'How was work?'

'Aw, you know, the usual meaningless drivel.'

I asked her if their mother had called. She had not. I made a start at dinner, which was easy—leftover pasta with chilli sauce. I put the chilli sauce in a pan on the stove and then called Fiona's mobile phone. She picked up and I could hear the engine of her car.

'Hi, Michael, I'm almost home.'

I told her dinner was a work in progress. Then she asked me, 'Are Maebh and Francesca there?'

'Yeah… they're fine. Are *you* okay?'

Then she sounded vague.

'Nothing, no, I just, I'm fine, I just thought I saw Francesca on the street with some *fellow*—nothing—it must've been someone else. I'll be home in a minute.'

She hung up and I went upstairs. Francesca's room was empty. Her bed was covered up. I pulled the covers down. It was very warm. It had definitely been occupied during the last hour.

I called Maebh. She came out of her room and looked in at me in Francesca's.

'Where's Fran?'

'I thought *you* could throw some light on that topic?'

She shrugged. 'She was here a while ago. She was playing that Snow Patrol album—*loud*.'

I didn't want any more cover stories from Maebh. I said, 'Okay,' and she went back to her own room. I heard Fiona coming in downstairs; I went down and met her in the kitchen.

The chilli sauce was bubbling over on the stove. Fiona turned it down.

'You were right about Francesca—she's not here,' I said.

She shrugged her shoulders and picked up a casserole dish. She looked at me.

'She was *with* someone.'

Maebh came into the kitchen and said, 'Where's Fran?'

We didn't answer. Maebh pushed a few buttons on her mobile and we heard Francesca's mobile phone ringing somewhere upstairs. I looked at Maebh, '*You* know where she is?'

'I don't know—I am *not* my sister's keeper.'

That was helpful.

'Has she a boyfriend?' I asked.

Maebh shrugged again and said, 'I—I *doubt* it. She's *thirteen*, Dad.'

We heard the front door creaking open. Fiona looked out along the hall.

'Hey, Fran, where *were* you?'

Francesca came into the kitchen.

'What's up?'

I caught a glimpse of Maebh giving Francesca a *you're in trouble* shake of the head and dirty look. Francesca pretended not to see it. She stood behind one of the kitchen chairs and asked what was for dinner. I didn't answer. I put four plates on the table and opened the cutlery drawer.

In my head I was saying, 'Francesca, do you know what contraception is?'

My wife said, 'Let's eat.'

Francesca's phone rang; she ran out of the kitchen and upstairs to get it. She came back quickly and sat down.

'Who was that?' I asked.

Francesca said, 'Nobody,' and frowned at her plate.

'The same *nobody* you were dealing with downtown today?'

Francesca put down her fork. 'What the hell *is* this, the CIA or something? It's a free country, Dad. I can hang out with whoever I want.'

I put my own fork down.

'Young lady, you're wrong there. When you're eighteen you'll have the freedom to hook up with whoever you want. Until then you are in our charge, and no, you're *not* free. There's a lot you don't know.'

Fran stood up, she said, 'Oh, you think so?' and left the room. As she stomped down the hall she shouted back, 'There's a lot *you* don't know, Dad!'

The front door slammed. Francesca had left the building.

*

We had two of my wife's colleagues, Carolyn and Una, over for dinner last Thursday night. We decided to have a barbecue. I was grilling the burgers and chicken when fumes from the barbecue blew into the kitchen and set off the smoke alarm. I dragged my offending smoke machine to the other side of the back yard.

Fiona came across to me and said,

'It's getting a bit cold, so we'll set the table indoors.'

She went back in and I could see them through the kitchen window. My wife's back was to me and Carolyn was on her right hand side. Una seemed to be talking. I finished up the barbecuing and went into the kitchen for a second plate. As I got inside, Una was saying, 'We almost need a new specialty.'

'Everything okay, Michael?' Fiona asked.

I got the plates and went back out.

When I came back in I asked them what the new specialty was. Fiona, in her inimical back-in-your-box-Michael fashion, said, '*What?*' as if some stray dog had wandered in and asked a question about quantum mechanics.

'Gynaecology for girls,' Una said. 'Things are not like they were in *our* young days, Michael—it's the end of the world as we know it!'

Una and I were in the same class in secondary school.

'That patient has two different infections—STDs,' Fiona said. 'She hasn't even done her Junior Cert. yet. That's a first in my book.'

Carolyn said, 'Some young fellows made serious money building and when there's enough cash around it's all drugs and booze, and once these young girls—these babies—hanging around them get high enough, they'll do *anything*.'

'Celtic Tiger sex kittens,' Una said.

My wife shook her head, 'They might as well be turning tricks!'

Francesca's behaviour those weeks was completely consistent with this latest data on teenagers. I couldn't stand the idea of my own thirteen-year-old daughter messing around like that.

And last week I spotted her. I deliberately parked in the centre of town near the phone shop and waited. And sure enough I saw her with some overweight gorilla going into McDonald's.

I did not follow them. I started the car and went home.

That Saturday I wanted to fix the gutters on the house. I started at around nine in the morning and worked solidly all morning. At around three o'clock that afternoon I was up the ladder at the southern side of the house, and what did I see from my lofty vantage point but the bold Fran walking down the street with her big leather jacket yob of a *bucko* in tow. They came in off the street as bold as brass, went right in the front door and slammed it behind them.

I heard their footsteps as they went upstairs inside. I was livid. I could feel the blood vessels pulsing in my head. I got down the ladder, went in through the garage and crept up the stairs. I could hear their voices in Fran's room. Snow Patrol playing on the stereo: *If I lay here, if I just lay here, would you lie with me and just forget the world?*

I wanted to smash that big bastard's head in. I gripped the claw hammer in my right hand, held it up and swung her bedroom door open.

She was sitting on her bed and the offending John was sitting too. At the computer.

'Hello, *Dad*?' Fran said.

The young stud looked around at me. He did *not* look like a plasterer *or* a bricklayer or anything else. He looked like a thirteen-year-old boy—a bit overweight—with his school uniform on, which I thought was a bit *sad* on a Saturday.

He pushed back from the computer and glanced at the hammer. There was something about diabetes on the screen.

'Dad, this is Denis from my class,' Francesca said. 'He's just using my computer. Broadband. Are you *okay*, Dad?'

Denis held out his right hand. I put the hammer on the bed but it fell to the floor. I shook his hand in both of mine. I said, 'Denis, you're good, Denis, good. You're *very* good, thanks be to *Jesus*! Um, I was looking for the bathroom.'

I backed out the door.

Francesca came out after me.

'Dad, your hammer.'

I turned back up towards her on the stairs. She held out the hammer to me and I looked up at her face.

'*What the hell is wrong, Dad?*' she whispered.

When she released the hammer I stared at it in my hands. For a second I didn't know what I was supposed to do with it. Then her shoes came into focus. I wanted to talk to her, but I was looking at her shoes.

FAKE

RADU PAVEL GHEO

Translated from the Romanian by Philip Ó Ceallaigh

It had cooled down a little outside. The village was deep in darkness and nobody much was about, except for the five kids by the roadway in front of Dorinel's house. Three sat on the wooden bench and two crowded onto a mound of sand next to it. Soon a sixth arrived.

'Is he here yet?' asked the newcomer.

'Not yet,' replied one of the boys on the bench. 'I spoke to Grandad Gheorghe.'

'Well, where's he got to?' asked a fat blond boy on the bench.

'Who the hell knows,' said the dark-haired boy beside him, shrugging like a grown-up.

'Maybe he's with Ioana,' suggested a third boy.

'Yeah, that's it...' agreed the others.

Dorinel, their friend, was about twenty and had been 'seeing' Ioana since getting out of the army. All this was back when the army was compulsory for boys, Romania was a Socialist Republic led by Nicolae Ceausescu, when there was still a Federated Socialist Republic of Yugoslavia and the Soviet Union was trying to keep up with the United States in what was called the Cold War. Except that none of the six boys in front of Dorinel's house really understood any of that, and none of it existed any more by the time they understood. At that moment, though, what they did understand was that it was Friday evening, which meant that on Yugoslav television, on channel two, there would be *one of those films*. And it's easy to imagine what's meant by *one of those films* in a country where the national television station was on air for two hours per day, and the most erotic image that could be seen was a metre-long skirt.

Dorinel was still unemployed that summer and had nothing to do but hang around the village, which was how he had come to adopt the five boys and stay up late with them watching 'Serb' television or playing cards for matchsticks. Dorinel had a special aerial, made in a workshop in the city, that just about picked up the signal for TV2 Belgrade.

The young man shared the family home with only his grandfather Gheorghe. Dorinel's mother had died when he was ten. Five years later his father had remarried with a widow from the village and for a while had two households. Then, when Dorinel got out of the army, he moved out and in with the woman. So, Dorinel's house was the sole place where the eroticism transmitted from across the border could be explored without risk.

Much later, after midnight, Dorinel appeared, whistling gently. The boys stood up and gathered around him.

'Hello, Dorinel! Hello!'

'Well! Aren't you in bed yet? What will your parents say?'

He was only fooling with them, talking like that.

'We're on holidays, Dorinel,' muttered one of the boys.

'Sure you are,' nodded Dorinel. 'And you want to watch television, isn't that it?'

'Well, yeah... it's Friday night, isn't it?'

'Friday night, it is indeed.'

Dorinel unlocked the gate, still whistling, the six boys crowding in after him. Then he crossed the yard, with the boys stumbling quietly along and entering the house one by one. They stopped in the hall and removed their shoes. Then they entered the room with the television and sprawled out where they could on the carpet, leaving Dorinel the best place: the wide bed with the enormous quilt.

'Hasn't it started already?' said a boy with close-cropped hair.

Dorinel sniggered. 'Can't wait to see some bare tits! Relax, it's early, not even half-one.'

'Dorinel, here!' said another boy, the dark-haired one, handing him a pack of cigarettes. 'We got you a packet of Wikend, they're from Serbia.'

'Right-o.'

Dorinel took the cigarettes and put them next to him, on the bedside locker. Then he got up, went over to the television, facing them on a low table, and turned it on.

A fuzzy black and white picture slowly appeared, full of static and with a loud whine instead of sound, so Dorinel began slowly twisting the tuner. He worked at that for a bit, to no great effect. The boys stared tensely.

'Hey, Florin, go on out and play with the aerial. I think the wind knocked it the wrong way last night.'

Florin—the chubby blond boy—hurried out. In the yard, he positioned himself beside an iron mast like a flagpole atop which the aerial was attached. Meanwhile, following a well-established ritual, another boy stood in the corridor and a third in the doorway of the room. They waited for the signal.

'Turn it!'

'Turn it!' shouted the boy in the doorway.

'Turn it!' shouted the one in the corridor.

Florin revolved the aerial a little.

'More!'

The message was passed along. More! More!

The pole supporting the aerial squeaked sharply. The picture improved greatly.

'A bit more!' said Dorinel.

'A bit more!'

Another short squeak, stopped by a shout from Dorinel:

'Stop!'

'Stop!'

'Stop!'

Now it was fine. The black and white picture had settled down, was fairly sharp, and the sound was very good. A music video was playing.

'Look!' said the dark-haired boy. 'The new Madonna song!'

The other five crowded more closely around the screen. Dorinel withdrew, shrugging. He liked traditional music. The foreign stuff the kids listened to on Yugoslav radio and television left him cold. But he too wanted to see the two o'clock film.

Two o'clock finally came and, after a slew of ads for enticing products—jeans, soft drinks, chocolate, beautiful cars—the long awaited film began. It was about a doctor for women in the Place Pigalle who received all kinds of patients who were hungry for sex or wanted their breasts enlarged, and the doctor took care of them all. He also took care of his two nurses. He took care of his patients in turn, or together, with or without the help of the nurses, and sometimes with the help of the husband of one of the patients.

The seven viewers had gone silent, glued to the screen, trying to memorise every image. Dorinel lit up a Wikend and puffed on it greedily. From time to time the faces illuminated on the bluish screen let out little yelps or moans, such as when a woman on her own used an empty Cola bottle in an unusual way, twisting it between her thighs while a maid and a valet watched her through a door left ajar and felt each other up.

'Coca-Cola!' whispered one of the boys.

'Shut up, Petrica!' hissed Florin, the fat blond boy.

The room reverberated with the moans and gasps of the actors. And just as the action on the screen was approaching a climax, the creak of the door opening was heard. The boys started, as though woken from a trance.

'What's up, Grandad, can't sleep again?'

'Again, Grandson.'

Dressed only in long johns tied with a drawstring and a faded old pyjama top with three different kinds of buttons, Grandad Gheorghe slowly entered the room.

'What are all these kids doing here? Where'd you get them from?'

'They're here to see a Serb film.'

'What film?'

'A porno film, Grandad Gheorghe,' said one of the boys.

Grandad Gheorghe slowly shuffled over to the bed and sat down. He too watched for a bit, elbows on his knees, chin resting in his palms. The boys concentrated on the television but felt rather uncomfortable: Dorinel was one of the lads, but Grandad Gheorghe was a grown-up. Who knew what went on in his head? And indeed, the old man eventually said:

'Now, children, why are you sitting up at night like fools watching this rubbish? Don't you have school?'

'We're on holidays, Grandad Gheorghe,' said the dark-haired boy, in an appeasing voice.

'Let them be, Grandad. They'll learn something about women,' said Dorinel easily, lighting another cigarette.

'Learn what?' asked Grandad Gheorghe, gently. 'Pass me a cigarette there, Grandson.'

Dorinel handed him a Wikend and a box of matches. After he'd smoked a bit and followed the film steadily, the old man spoke up again:

'Learn what? This is all, what do you call it? Tricks... faked... It's all fake, dear children!'

'How can it all be fake, Grandad Gheorghe?' mumbled Florin.

'Trust me, I know,' replied the old man confidently. 'You think they'd put something like that on television if it was real?'

'Well, why not?' asked Florin, surprised. 'There, look. They're showing it.'

'They're showing it because it's faked,' sighed the old man. 'That's how it is with television.'

Nobody said anything. A black man had appeared on the screen, standing on a table, his back curved to such a degree that his lips were able to reach to between his legs.

'See? It's faked,' insisted Grandad Gheorghe. 'When have you ever seen a normal person doing that kind of thing?'

Just then the screen darkened and died.

'Damn it to hell!' exclaimed Dorinel. 'Another blackout! At this hour! Damn them anyway!'

The village suffered frequent power cuts as part of the national programme for saving energy, but there had never been one at such a late hour. Usually it happened in the evening, around seven or eight, when people were back from work and presumably wasting energy around the house.

'Ah, doesn't matter,' muttered Grandad Gheorghe. 'Dorinel, there's a candle behind the television.'

Dorinel lit the candle, and they all sat there, waiting. Perhaps it wouldn't last long. Perhaps they'd catch the end of the film.

'Dear children, you're wasting your time watching that,' resumed Grandad Gheorghe. 'It's not real. That's not how it's done with women.'

'But if it's there, on television…' argued Florin, with a note of uncertainty in his voice.

'So what if it's on television? What, haven't you seen talking mice on television? Haven't you seen how nice Ceausescu is on television? It's fake, children! It's not real.'

'And how do you know for sure, Grandad Gheorghe?' asked the boy with the close-cropped hair.

'Oh, come on! I'm eighty years old and I've had dealings with women in their bare skin. Have any of you ever undressed one? Or even seen a woman naked?'

The boys were silenced by the directness of the question.

'Well, maybe we have!' piped up one of the boys behind Florin.

'Really? Well then, tell this old man one thing: is a blonde woman blonde down below too?'

'Yeah, she's blonde there too!' asserted Florin.

'Really?' laughed Grandad Gheorghe.

'No, the hair's black down there!' volunteered another boy.

'Oh, children, children!' sighed Grandad Gheorghe, amused. 'There's still a whiff of pussy off you, it seems. But you don't know the first thing about it. You, you're Gheorghe Mada's boy, aren't you?' he asked Florin.

'Yes,' replied Florin, timidly.

'Then go ask your old grandad, while he's still around, what women are like down below, since he knows better than any man in the village.'

'Really?' asked Florin, surprised, with a trace of pride. 'How's that?'

'Well, before the war he was a barber for women in the city.'

'What do you mean, barber for women?' asked Florin, astounded.

'Just that. He trimmed them, below, so it would be nice and neat to the touch when a man reached down. Oh, children, children!'

Then the television crackled and the picture slowly returned. Dorinel blew out the candle and everybody gathered around again. The action continued onscreen and each of the seven had the impression that they had missed almost nothing—or, at the very least, that they were picking up where they had left off.

Grandad Gheorghe stood up and said:

'Well, I'm off to bed, Grandson. And you, Florin, don't forget tomorrow to talk to your grandfather, who's older and wiser. And don't be believing that fake Serbian rubbish.'

Grandad Gheorghe remained convinced that the films the kids crowded in to watch on Friday evenings were faked and nobody could ever persuade him otherwise. How could you really put something like that on television? And not so long after that Ceausescu ceased to exist, and Yugoslav television ceased to exist, and at about the same time Grandad Gheorge ceased to exist too. And the boys found out the truth about blonde women. And they drank hundreds of bottles of Coca-Cola. These things and many others have started to seem normal and, as is inevitable, much less interesting than the fake things seen back then, in Dorinel's crowded room.

THE GIRL IN THE WINDOW
BRIAN KIRK

She stands at the third floor window and looks across at me, as she has done every morning this week. On Monday and Tuesday I watched her idly, but on Wednesday I stood and leaned my face against the glass, my stifled breath forming a tight ball in my chest that, when released, clouded the pane. She must have seen me watching her. Today she stands in the window yet again, and this time she undresses. Slowly. For me. I am careful not to fog the glass this time.

I have taken to closing my office door lately, but it makes no difference—they never knock anyway. They are talking, asking a question, before I can even see their faces. It is assumed I am all right with this. I am not. Perhaps I should bawl them out the way my predecessors would have done. When I started in the bank twenty-five years ago, even a middle manager like me was a god. Clerks didn't speak unless they were spoken to, and you never entered an office without knocking and receiving an invitation to enter. Of course we don't call them clerks any more; these days everyone must have a flattering job title.

Back then there was no such thing as regulation, or risk management, or corporate governance. We, on the investment side of the house, relied on our guts; we took chances to make money, for the bank, for the client, for ourselves. But we had our own unwritten rules. To be honest, I have never really understood these new nebulous terms. I have a vague notion of what they might mean, but I don't need or care to know. I have staff who I can assign to these areas if I need to from the haven of my office. Lately I try to avoid face to face interaction altogether if I can. I was never what they call a people person; I much preferred working with numbers. A well designed graph can tell me far more about a stock's prospects in a couple of seconds than endless stammering presentations can in an hour. People can't help themselves, they exaggerate, embellish, take liberties with the truth. But figures don't lie. You just have to keep watching the numbers, following the trends, that's all.

To be honest, I generally dislike people. I find it a challenge these days just to walk through the office, among the open plan desks, towards the toilets. There is always someone who wants to engage you in conversation. As if I would be interested in their surfing weekend in Lahinch or the efforts of their slobbering toddler to create sounds that may or may not be actual words.

So I remain in my office with the door shut, sit on my leather swivel chair with my back to the desk, a report open on my lap, and I gaze out the window. My office is on the third floor and affords a sweeping view along a wide street perpendicular to one of the main thoroughfares of the city. Across the road is a hostel for young backpackers, a modish bar, a café, a beauty salon, and the hotel where I watch as the beautiful girl undresses. Did I mention how beautiful she is? No? Strange. I think of Imelda, my wife, the excess of pink stippled flesh on the underside of her upper arms, the sag of her stomach, and I have to admit that my girl is exquisite.

Nose pressed to the glass, breath held, I watch her undress, in quiet panic. Will the door open? Will my boss come in? Roger, the boss who is younger than me, the one who got the directorship that I was expected to get four years ago because he knew and cared about such things as risk management and corporate governance? Will I make a joke of it?

I know Roger no longer cares about me or what I do. But he is not a fool. He knows I have lost interest in the work, he notices that I no longer speak at the management meetings. I saw the way he looked through me at the crisis meeting last Monday morning. He spoke dolefully of global losses on the markets, of the importance of watching the trends, of spreading the risk for our investors, of the possibility of a competitor going under. He let that thought hang in the air for a while for effect and was rewarded with a grave penitent murmur from my colleagues.

Monday morning again. I take the early train to work and arrive just as the porter is opening the building. I make myself some coffee, delighting in the silence, the peace. I spin in my chair to face the window, polishing my glasses carefully before standing at the glass. Her curtains are drawn. Outside the closed door of my office I can hear the early starters arriving, exchanging hellos. I sip my coffee, stare at the window and will her to appear. Steam from the cup clouds the lenses of my glasses and I set about carefully wiping them again. When I return to the window, her curtains are open. There she is, in the back of the room, hardly more than a shadow. I move closer to the window, making myself as visible as possible, and stay there, knowing she watches for me, that she wants me to see her.

On Friday last Roger came into my office. Fortunately I was not at the window. He spoke about changes, about new challenges in a constricting economy, about tough decisions. He didn't say it directly, but we both knew my career was almost over.

All weekend I thought about the girl in the window. I tried to focus on the prospect of losing my job, but I couldn't, my mind wouldn't move from the memory of her naked image framed in a sash window one hundred feet away. I went to the golf club annual dinner dance with Imelda on Saturday night and drank a little too much. She brought me home early and was uncommonly tender as she made tea and helped me up the stairs to bed. The next morning when I woke the girl's illicit image filled my mind immediately and I was aroused. I rose as quietly as I could, head hurting a little, and went to the bathroom to pee. Nothing came, so I set myself difficult mathematical problems in an effort to divert my thoughts and finally managed to pass water, before tiptoeing quickly back to bed. Imelda stirred briefly. I shut my eyes tight and welcomed the girl's image again. Unaccountably, my wife turned to me then and kissed me as I pretended to sleep. I was momentarily annoyed by the interruption, but I soon realised from the insistence of her attention that she was asking for reciprocation. I kept my eyes firmly closed, caressing the girl's splendid form in my mind, taking her in my arms, tasting her lips, making her moan. All day Imelda tried her best to fuss and be attentive, but the girl's image never left my mind for a second.

We never had children. Now it is too late for us, even to adopt. We rattle around in a detached mock Tudor house in an exclusive estate of detached mock Tudor houses in the middle of nowhere. There is a village two miles away, but the roads are so narrow and dangerous you have to take the car everywhere. We are thrown together, Imelda and I, for two days every week, and a routine has developed where we hardly have to speak to each other at all. We read the newspapers, or our books, watch the TV, and sometimes we go out, to the golf club or the hotel for a meal or a few drinks in the hope we might meet someone else we can talk to.

At last she appears at the window, wearing a white bathrobe, a white towel corkscrewed on her head. She looks out across the distance to me and I hold her gaze, no longer afraid to let her see that I am there, that I am watching her. Slowly she removes the towel and, bending slightly, dries her slick, black hair. She tosses the towel aside and moves a little closer to the window, gazing at me, her hands deliberately undoing the belt of her robe and letting the robe fall. I know it sounds stupid, but I love her, silently watching her naked body. I feel grateful to her, whoever she is, that she should choose to share her beauty with me.

'She's one dirty bitch, isn't she?'

It is Roger's voice at my shoulder.

'The guys on the floor were talking about her early morning show all last week—thought I'd check it out myself. They reckoned you'd have the best vantage point from here. They weren't wrong I see, you sly old dog, you!'

She must be able to see him by my side. She moves away, and I turn to face him.

'Get out of my office,' I say calmly, because I finally know what I am doing.

'What?'

'I said, get out of my office before I throw you out. I'm giving you notice, one month from today, and then you won't have to see me again.'

Roger looks at me. He really looks at me for the first time in years I think, and I believe he does not recognise what he sees. From the moment I stopped being a productive member of the team I had ceased to exist for him, but now I am suddenly made flesh again before his eyes. He looks back once more as he leaves the office. I think he is actually frightened of me, and I am heartened by the thought.

'There's no need to work your notice. You can leave right now if you want.'

He stops with a hand on the door handle.

'You haven't worked in years anyway, have you?'

He shuts the door—he doesn't slam it—in his wake.

I begin to empty my desk drawers. Not surprisingly, there is little I want to keep. When I have put my coat on I stand with my briefcase in hand by the window. Watching. Eventually she comes and stands looking out at me. Not through me, but at me. I wonder does she think I am just the same as the others, the men who stand at the window and watch her. I hope she sees me differently.

She is fully dressed now, in a dark top and pale knee length skirt. Her black hair shines in the mid-morning sunlight, and she strokes it self-consciously as I watch her. I raise my right hand briefly. She returns my salute, then she turns away for good.

FIVE STORIES

ALEX EPSTEIN

Translated from the Hebrew by Becka Mara McKay

THE CRIPPLED ANGEL

The crippled angel sat in a wheelchair especially designed for winged creatures of his kind and chain smoked. From his usual spot in the plaza in front of the museum, he observed with concern those coming in. He tried to guess which one of them intended to hang himself in one of the exhibition halls.

JUNG'S NIGHTMARE OF WATCHES

Except for one sentence pierced by the explicit word 'reality,' almost nothing of what will be told here happened in the distant summer of 1926, when Karl Jung, the psychoanalyst, gave his mistress a gift: a wristwatch without a minute hand. He asked her to wear it even in her sleep, because this watch, so he said, measures the time of love.

A few days later, Jung's mistress bumped into Jung's wife, who stood examining the window display of a paint-supply shop on a Zurich boulevard. The two women, who had already met once at a party, shook hands politely. Jung's mistress couldn't help noticing that on her wrist, Mrs Jung wore a watch that had no hour hand. This encounter certainly had consequences in reality, though reality, as is well known, is paler than its own shadow. In any case, in one of Jung's dreams the two women also asked each other for the time.

HOMER'S CHILDHOOD GAMES

Nor will this story have enough room to answer the question of what is so true about a true story. According to one version, Homer lost his sight at the age of two. According to another version, he was blind from birth. At the age of six, over the course of long months, he learned the rules of chess, the terrain of the board and the shapes of the pieces; how to make an opening move without looking and then without feeling his way. Of course, chess had not been invented in those days—this needs to be told in another way: in childhood he had already learned to unravel the braid of January's last rain into the threads of a dozen plots. But January also had yet to appear. Nor will an answer to the question of what is the story in a true story be found here. Like many blind storytellers, already in his childhood Homer knew, without looking at the heavens, when the moon waned, and when it filled.

MORE ON THE RETURN OF ODYSSEUS

He never told her that he once woke up above the ocean without a shred of a memory of who he was. When he landed he adjusted to local time the watch that he wore on his right hand (although he didn't feel left-handed), passed the border inspection, and began collecting information about his life: his name on a passport under an outdated photo, his unshaven face reflected in the restroom mirror, his address in a telephone book, the gifts for his children in a suitcase (he tried in vain to open the packages so that he'd be able to close them again), the cigarette he hadn't managed to finish on the sidewalk outside the terminal, the rainy landscape out the window on the cab ride home. His voice was strange to him, but he tried his best to keep it from breaking when he opened the apartment door with the key he found in his coat pocket and said: 'I'm here,'—at that moment he hoped in vain that nobody would be there, and he would have more time to get to know them better—'it's me.'

TIME WAR

The war broke out a year ago in July. The first attack occurred immediately after we built a time machine and made contact with the future. Our great-grandchildren from the 22nd century attacked us with ground-time-ground missiles. The missiles fell simultaneously on the outskirts of Milan and in the heart of Florence and caused heavy damage.

We tried to understand: If they destroyed some of us, their ancestors, they would destroy themselves. A few physicists, who had promised us that time travel would be as safe as driving down an empty road, now asked for some time so they could study the behaviour of the variables, to find the cause and effect. (This is not necessarily a paradox, they said. Maybe what we should learn from this is that the butterfly effect impacts the timeline as well. What appears to us as a crazy whim is liable to appear in another one or two hundred years as a tiny stone in a magnificent mosaic of time.) But after nearly all of Paris was destroyed in a single night in a shower of hundreds of cruise missiles, we decided that this was not the time to stop and ponder.

We responded with decisive force. We sent commando units into the future, to strike at the communication centres of our great-grandchildren. Their reaction didn't take long: stealth bombers dropped neutron bombs on New York and Washington. We recruited one hundred suicide bombers carrying dirty bombs and sent them to their Moscow. They answered with a weapon we didn't know existed, a ray that burned, directly from the year 2146, Los Angeles, New Delhi, London, and half of Japan. We found a way to send unmanned jets to the future and bombed our great-grandchildren with our entire atomic arsenal. The scouts we sent to the future reported that the damage we caused to our great-grandchildren was noticeable, but the monuments that we had yet to build to the victims of their attacks on our time were countless. And indeed, they responded with a broad offensive on Northern Europe, Australia, and the Middle East.

We put our trust in the past. We prepared escape plans for children and the elderly. Entire nursing homes and orphanages were moved to unsettled areas in the Americas of 1412. And then, at the end of many months of warfare, we gained an unexpected ally. The great-grandchildren of our great-grandchildren from the 23rd century signed a treaty with us. They had a doomsday weapon. Half of the planet of our great-grandchildren was obliterated. Our enemies had no other option. They signed the agreement of surrender and left this century in peace. (Now the night is quiet and warm at the end of July. Far from here, in Buenos Aires or in Cairo, someone puts on an old record that he hasn't heard in years. I wonder if the record will still play, he asks himself. Someone else, in Rome or in Lisbon, turns out the light in the children's room. In Chicago, perhaps morning is breaking. In Seoul, perhaps it is raining. In Berlin or in Belgrade, in St Petersburg or in Cape Town, in Dublin or in Jerusalem, here or anywhere, you are still sitting at the desk in the study and searching, maybe in vain, for the words that will begin the letter to your unborn son.)

BLIZZARD

ANDREW FOX

The night is dry as Adam punches his timecard at the warehouse but a blizzard breaks while he is jammed on the BQE and by the time he reaches Woodside the snow has stuck. The neighbourhood doesn't know itself. All along the length of Roosevelt Avenue apartment buildings and storefronts gleam as though they might always have been this beautiful. On the sidewalk deep footprints describe a dance long finished or predict one about to begin.

Adam locks the truck and starts to walk with heavy steps. He is tired. For fourteen hours he has been making airport runs for Celtic Couriers, carrying thick sheaves of express letters, fragile parcels, rattling boxes—this is the height of the Christmas rush and he has been glad of the overtime. His building is a five-storey walk-up in the shadow of the elevated train tracks on the corner of Thirty-ninth Avenue, with steep front steps signed by *Enriqu*—whose piss ran out too quickly—and a sticking street door: a slow push and pull of key and worn lock to the tune of the 7 train's clatter. In the hallway Adam stops and makes sure that his phone is on, in case she calls. And he checks his watch: getting late.

In the apartment the lights are on and the murmur of the TV suggests that Steo might still be awake. Adam pulls back the curtain that they have hung for privacy and finds his roommate, still curled on his mattress, shivering away the night after his fifth straight day off work. The room is cold and dirty: hiss of a weak radiator and evidence

63

of sickness in sweat-smelling bedclothes and stacks of plates.

'How's the patient?'

'Sick as a fucking hospital.'

Steo's eyes are dark and his hair is greasy. Construction work has made his body hard, but it is a hardness from shrinking rather than from growth: his arms are rippled with muscle but very thin; his flat stomach and wide chest look brittle through a threadbare Dublin jersey.

'Looks like the snow's sticking, anyway,' Adam says. 'The Downstairs Giant's been out and you wouldn't believe the Frankenstein footprints.'

'I'd believe it, I'd believe it.' Steo struggles to sit. He looks around the room as if suddenly lost. 'Here, what time is it anyway? You're late.'

'Nearly midnight.'

'I was starting to think the *federales* had got you.'

There is a rocking chair wedged between the wall and Steo's mattress. It is the apartment's only real piece of furniture, stolen by Steo from the sidewalk outside an antiques store a week after he moved in. Adam sits in it now, and together they settle in to watch TV.

'What'd you do in here all day, anyway?'

'Tried not to die. I haven't even had the energy to wank myself.'

Adam rocks forward and looks at Steo from the tops of his eyes.

'Well, once. But it nearly fucking killed me.'

Between TV shows commercials hawk pills for heart conditions, night blindness, erectile dysfunction and deep vein thrombosis. Couples dance together, walk together with their dogs on long beaches, while a voice-over confesses to side effects. Steo watches the ads closely, and Adam watches him, knowing what will come next.

'I think I need to see a doctor.'

'You're grand.'

'Can you lend me—'

'You're grand.'

'I'm serious.'

'I'm skint—'

'Then what good are you?'

'—from covering your rent.'

The radiator's hiss breaks out into a shrill whistle. Adam goes to it, hunkers down, and beats the bullet-shaped steam valve with the stone Buddha kept for that purpose. The Buddha was a moving-in gift for Karen from the landlady, Mrs Hwang. 'It will keep you safe from unlucky dragons,' she had said.

The radiator gurgles as air moves through its pipes. On the back of his neck Adam feels a chill from the open window.

'Jesus, it's fucking Baltic in here, man. Can we not close that, no?'

'Look,' Steo says, 'Adam, I want an answer, *now*. No more dancing around it. Have you made up your mind yet? Are you staying or are you going or what?'

'I told you: I don't know.'

The underside of the frame is lumpy with ice to Adam's touch. He tugs at it, pushes it, slams it with the palm of his hand. He picks up the Buddha and hammers at the frame, splintering old wood and crisp paint and shaking insect carcasses from their rest in the raised net screen. But the frame won't budge. Adam drops the Buddha to the floor.

'The thing's painted open. Who ever heard of a window being painted open? We'll have to get Hwang-o to sort it out tomorrow. We can't live like this.'

Adam's phone rings. Steo shivers and curls more tightly beneath his blankets, watching from the corner of his eye as Adam answers then searches for a pen and writes on the back of his hand.

'Yeah. I'll be there.' Adam hangs up. 'Guess who?'

'Where is she so?' Steo's grin shows two rows of sharp teeth.

'The city.'

'Well, fair play to the girl. She must be moving up.'

Adam edges the truck out of Woodside onto Queens Boulevard and takes the Queensboro Bridge. As the truck climbs he feels the usual tightening in his chest and, high above the East River, experiences a moment of terrified weightlessness before being propelled down into the fifties and the madness of Manhattan traffic.

The first time he made one of these trips he had felt like a hero. That was three weeks after Karen had left him: three weeks during which he hadn't heard a word. When he answered the phone he heard crying. She was stranded, she said, and scared. With only her vague notion of where she might be to guide him, he had rushed out into the night, and found her hours later, having driven what felt like every street in Lower Manhattan. Eventually he got it out of her that she had closed the bar and gone to a club with a regular customer, who gave her ecstasy and took her home and then put her out on the street. Driving that night, with Karen clinging to him in the passenger seat, Adam had felt that everything might be okay. But the next morning she was gone.

From the high cab of the truck he can see out over the stretch of cars ahead: red lights growing faint in the distance and the stream of yellow taxis. He checks his directions and guides the truck downtown, away from the straight-line avenues of Midtown into the confusion of Tribeca. He finds the street: a quiet, empty, glass-sided canyon floored with steaming subway grates. And he finds Karen, standing under an awning with a fat little doorman in full livery, who holds an umbrella above her head. The doorman waves and Adam waves back, suddenly grateful that there is a witness to this small event, someone to see Karen run towards his truck and get in.

Karen breathes hard as she brushes snow from her shoulders. Without meeting Adam's eye she tells him: 'You're a sweetheart.'

'You know it's no problem.'

'Few left like ye, but. Not like that cunt in there. That fucker wouldn't even pay for a cab.'

Her smell is a mixture of sweat, new perfume, old smoke and alcohol. 'Jesus,' Adam says, 'you're drunk.'

The truck makes slow progress on the West Side Highway, its wipers straining and its tyres fighting snow. In silence they move beneath the tangle of ramps that feed the Port Authority bus station. They pass the Forty-second Street train garage, and block after block of shabby streets lit by the neon bulbs of strip bars and the marquees of off-off Broadway. On the far side of the river the lights of Jersey hum dimly, the outlines of the buildings there ghostly and uncertain. In Riverside Park, drunken teenagers are throwing snowballs built around rocks: the stricken go down and stay put.

'I can't keep doing this, Karen.'

'But you do keep doing it.'

'No, I mean, I don't mind doing it, but my licence is nearly up. And our visas are up. I'm not sure I should even be here any more.'

'Well, you'll suit yourself. You always have, always do.'

As he parks the truck in front of Karen's building, Adam feels a cold hand settle over his own. Karen cries a little as she kisses his cheek, and despite himself he concentrates on the new foreignness of her smell, the newly dyed hair, the coldness of her skin.

McLean Avenue disappears slowly as the windshield clouds with the fog of their breath and heat. Adam wipes a portal in the glass with his sleeve and looks out at the last dregs, the sagging pubs and the grime in the falling snow. On the corner a bar is letting out and men, arm-in-arm, are spilling onto the sidewalk, laughing their way into a staggering kick-line or circling one another and throwing soft punches.

Karen roots in her bag for cigarettes. She lights one, offers the box to Adam, but he waves it away.

'Look: why don't you just come home, Karen?'

'I'm here.'

'Why don't you come *home* home?'

Karen's nostrils stream bitter smoke. 'Why do you keep giving me advice? If I want to stay, I'll stay.'

'I'm sorry.'

'Well, I suppose it can't be helped. You're absolved, okay? You've no reason to feel guilty.'

Adam leans forward to play with the heater, bending into a pain in his stomach. It is something old and raw: a feeling of love that is quickly turning or has already turned to hatred.

'Who said anything about guilt?'

Karen stubs out her half-finished cigarette and puts the butt in her coat pocket. She reaches out to lay a hand on the door handle.

'Listen,' Adam says. 'I'd stay if you wanted me to. If you thought you could…'

The door is open quickly, and Karen is out on the street. She bends back inside the truck, her hair falling over her face. She touches Adam's shoulder and is gone.

Back in Woodside Adam parks beneath the tracks at the Sixty-first Street train station and sits for a while in the warmth of the truck. Overhead a train trundles past, shaking clumps of snow and ice from the track's supporting lattice. Moments later, from the mouth of the station's stairway, a large, bulky man appears, powering through the snow. Adam gets out of the truck and calls to the Downstairs Giant, who waves and darts across the street, narrowly beating an unstoppable taxi. He falls into step beside Adam and breathes a deep '*Hola.*'

'Sweet Jesus,' Adam says. 'That cold'd fucking have you.'

The Giant radiates body-heat and the smell of breeze-block dust and whiskey. His eyes are red. He leans his head back to look into the sky and the snow as he walks.

'Are you half-cut?' Adam asks.

The Giant looks at him, blinking.

'Drunk? Are you drunk?'

'*Sí.* Drunk!' the Giant laughs. 'I come from my party. For my leaving.'

'Was that tonight?'

'*Sí.*'

'Christ, I'm sorry I missed it.'

'You had plans, maybe?'

'Something like that.'

The Giant stops to light a cigarette. Adam watches the huge hands work the lighter, like the operation might be keyhole surgery.

'How is the girl?' the Giant asks. 'Sorry I do not see her. I am used to see her. She was nice.'

'I know she was.'

'Sometimes she would buy for me coffee in the morning.'

'I didn't know that.'

Waiting at the crosswalk Adam watches his shoes sinking into the thick slush. A plough truck passes, orange lights rotating at its corners, and leaves a trail of salt. The Giant shakes his head. 'These things, they happen. But a woman, if she loves you, sometimes she will forgive.'

'This woman never forgives anything.'

Loud music is playing inside Sean Óg's. Two women stand in the doorway of the pub, their arms crossed against the cold, smoking cigarettes. The Giant points past them. 'Pint?' he says. 'I'll buy.'

Adam shakes his head. He jams his hands in his coat pockets. The cold air pulls at the corners of his eyes. 'I need to think.'

The Giant bends to hug Adam and Adam stretches up, his head to the Giant's chest and the great heart inside that pounds as loud as a marching drum.

'Well, good luck,' Adam says. 'And, if I don't see you—'

'I will see you. Sometime.'

'No,' Adam says. 'You won't.'

*

Hours later Adam sits on his bed, flipping through newspapers and magazines but reading no more than a few words. He thumbs the spines of his small collection of books but doesn't pick one out, counts his teeth with his tongue but comes up with contradictory numbers. Sean Óg's has spilled back to the Giant's apartment, and rising through the floorboards are the sounds of savage football songs competing for attention in English and Spanish. Adam knows that he will never get to sleep. He is thinking of a conversation he had with Steo on the day his visa ran out. They had known each other only a few months then, but already Steo had watched Adam leave many times—to pick Karen up, to help her move furniture, to argue with her landlord, to kill cockroaches—without ever asking questions. This night though, they had gotten drunk.

Steo asked: 'Why do you do it, Adam?'

'Because she needs me to.'

'No,' Steo said. 'She doesn't.'

Adam gets to his feet and walks to the door, closes it softly behind him and climbs the last flight of stairs to the roof. He feels no closer now to Karen than he did before he went to her, no further away than he will feel next week in Dublin. Outside there is a thick covering of snow. Manhattan's jagged horizon is dimly visible, its line rising out of the harbour and falling away towards the Bronx and Karen. In the street below the steady snow-cover swallows old footprints while new walkers add their own. Above the building countless snowflakes circle one another, and like that, for a long while, Adam sits to watch them dance.

THE MASTER PLAN
CHARLOTTE GRIMSHAW

Marcella opened the door. Thérèse, talking on her mobile, wrestled a small suitcase over the doorstep and kicked it into the hall. She tossed her blonde hair over her shoulder, leaned forward and kissed Marcella on the cheeks, one two three. She gave a furious shrug, hissed something, snapped the phone shut, turned back and hefted another bag through the door.

Thérèse was wearing a beautiful fine white coat, belted at her slim waist, and long black stiletto-heeled boots. She said, 'I'm so sorry. I know this is absolutely terrible of me, the short notice.'

Marcella said, 'It's fine. Honestly. Hugo will be pleased.' She pushed the small silver suitcase out of the way. 'Is this Michel's stuff?'

'I've shoved in his pyjamas and a toothbrush—God, did I put in a toothbrush?—anyway he's got jackets and things, underwear. I'm so sorry about this. Luc only told me he was going to Marseilles this morning. It's now or never.'

'Are you sure you should just take the painting? Not try to discuss?'

'Discuss? Are you joking? He'll never give it up. He says it's his. And it's mine. Okay, we were together when it was given to me, but it was given to me.'

Thérèse took out a brush and ran it through her hair. She smoothed and straightened her coat. She held out her hands and inspected her nails. 'He has never lifted a finger to help with Michel. He has been an absolute pig about my career. And now he wants to steal my painting. Or,' she stabbed a finger in the air, as if her ex-husband Luc were in the room, 'he wants to hold it to ransom, because he's thought up this notion that he should be able to see Michel whenever he wants, that I should have stayed in Paris, not brought him to London. He wants to keep me prisoner in some ghastly little apartment in Paris so he can pretend he sees his son, and then he won't, he'll be off with his insane girlfriend, he'll be playing tennis, he'll be getting up at noon . . .'

Marcella leaned against the wall, listening.

Thérèse tossed her head and sniffed. She rummaged in her bag, put on some lipstick.

Marcella said, 'Shall we have a coffee before you go?'

Thérèse kissed her again. 'No time. I'll be in Paris by the afternoon. It'll only take me a second to get the painting. I'll bring it back on the train. I'll ring you when I get there.'

Marcella said, 'I hope he hasn't changed the locks.'

'He won't have. He wouldn't know how to ring a locksmith. He's too intellectual. He's too effete.'

'Well. Ring me when you've got it.'

'I've got to be quick. He hates being out of Paris. I must get in before he comes back.'

She extended the handle on her dinky black bag and leaned across for one more kiss. She bumped the bag down the steps.

Marcella waved. 'Goodbye! *Bon chance!*'

The wind blew down the street, raising dust and leaves. She watched Thérèse walk away, swaying on her elegant heels, her blonde hair flying around her head. There was a hoarse shout from the men on the scaffolding across the road.

Thérèse twitched her narrow shoulders. She disappeared round the corner, towards the Tube. Silence. A tiny click from the thermostat. Shafts of weak sunlight came in through the window, making a pattern on the floor. Marcella wished Thérèse had stayed for a coffee.

I'm lonely, she thought, and she started to wonder about a dinner party. Something ambitious. She would cook an elaborate and difficult meal, duck perhaps, and invite too many people. She would fill the house. The idea pleased her. She made herself a cup of coffee and walked slowly upstairs to her study.

There was a new e-mail in her inbox. She paused, surprised. Richard Black. Her review of his new novel had just appeared in the *TLS*. Instead of opening the e-mail she shuffled through the pile on her desk and got out the piece. Reviewing made her nervous, but she accepted every book she was offered, determinedly, conscientiously. To have her name appear every so often in the *TLS* helped her get jobs as a freelance editor. She read the review. It was all right. Not too negative, just the odd quibble.

She opened the e-mail.

Marcella, I haven't seen you since you helped with that thing at Hay, but I still have your e-mail address. I've just read your review in the TLS. How can you imply I am a lazy, shallow writer, a once-over-lightly researcher? How can you imply I've just 'Googled' around my subject when everyone knows (ask Michaelson, ask John Stone, ask Jane Tiernan for God's sake) that I've been seriously interested in it since Oxford. Did you even read the novel? I have to ask. Because I wonder whether you have. And when you imply that I'm lazy and cynical, is that the case, or is it really your review that's all these things?

Fourteen years ago, when I began the first draft of Master *I was working on three other projects. I shelved the novel many times, but when I finally got on to it, it had been developing in my mind for a decade. I researched METICULOUSLY. I used to dream about it. And now, incredibly, you write a review in which you imply I've dashed the thing off in about three weeks, as if I needed the bloody advance . . .*

Marcella stood up and went to the window. She looked out at the dusty trees, the rooftops, the network of brick walls. In the distance the rumble of a train. She laughed nervously, played with a loop of her hair, said out loud, 'Shit.' She went to sit down and then jumped up again. 'Shit. Shit.'

She picked up the review, read it, then reread the e-mail. 'But this is ridiculous,' she said. 'Where? Google? Where did I say these things?'

She ran through the novel in her mind. What she really hadn't liked about it were the breathless descriptions of the narrator's wife. The young, beautiful, 'sassy' American, with her exquisite features, her fierce intelligence. Her multiple talents. Soprano, sex bomb, intellectual genius. Marcella had reflected, reading *The Master Plan*, that Richard Black used to be the most brilliant writer in England, but as soon as he'd divorced his English wife and got with that American, he'd lost his edge. He seemed to have put aside his sense of humour. At times he was positively syrupy. But she hadn't put any of these thoughts in the review. She hadn't mentioned the sentimentality. As far as his research went, she'd referred to it in passing, and quite neutrally. The review was disgracefully lenient!

She clicked Reply.

Dear Richard, I am stumped. Are you mixing me up with another reviewer? I haven't mentioned Google. I've barely mentioned your research. The only negative thing I can see in the piece is one word that might be construed as mocking, where I describe the narrator's relationship with his new wife. The word is 'throbbing'. Apart from that, I'm at a loss to understand what you're talking about. I am sorry if the review has upset you. But are you sure it's really as negative as you think? Marcella

She clicked Send. She thought about her ex-husband, Rob, in New York. He had an apartment there now. He had e-mailed, asking if she would send Hugo over for a visit, and she had refused. I am not sending my child over the Atlantic by himself. You left. If you want to see him, you come to us. He had rung her then. He had mentioned his 'rights'. 'You left,' she'd repeated. The conversation had turned bad. 'You have no rights,' she'd shouted, and hung up on him.

Marcella went downstairs and made another coffee. When she

came back, Richard Black had replied.

No, Marcella, I have not mixed up your review with another. Perhaps you've been reading the wrong novel? Thank you for calling the relationship between Marta and Julian 'throbbing'. All others who have read the book have described it as 'moving'. Richard.

I bet it was your new wife who told you it was moving, Marcella thought. She was irritated. She had work to do before she picked up the boys from school. Fucking arsehole, with his mid-life crisis and his sensitivities. Spoiled literary tyrant.

She clicked on Reply and typed,

I have work to do.

Her eyes burned suddenly. She brushed away tears.

I'm sorry if the review has annoyed you.

She pressed Send.

She really should have stuck up for herself. People had to take reviews on the chin; it was the only honourable thing to do. She blew her nose, and sat looking at the photo on her desk. Rob and Hugo on a beach in France. The father and son so alike, with their blue eyes.

The computer pinged. A reply flew in.

Your review isn't any good. It's badly written. It even contains a grammatical error, in line four. I woke this morning with a searing hangover and happened to pick up the TLS. My wife Cruz-Anne is in Peru, researching her second book on the Incas. I rang her but she wasn't in. Alone, badly, ineptly reviewed, I seriously contemplated a hair of the dog.

Marcella thought, What? Now out the window the trees swelled with wind, and birds rose and swooped across the gardens. She watched the birds. She reread his message. She stood at the window and pressed her palm against the glass. In the distance a woman opened a door and threw liquid out into her garden. The light caught it, a string of glass beads. Marcella was surrounded by silence.

Dear Richard, I read recently that Hans Christian Andersen was once found face down on the lawn at Gad's Hill Place, crying because he'd had

*a bad review. Dickens took him for a walk. He wrote 'criticism' in the dust
with his foot and then rubbed it out. He said, 'Never allow yourself to be
upset by the papers. They are forgotten in a week, but your work stands
and lives.'*

I also read that after Dickens wrote Bleak House *they said he wouldn't
last. That his talent was on the wane.*

But the book stood, didn't it.

So. Write my name in the dust and rub it out. Your work stands.
Marcella

She clicked Send. She tidied the papers on her desk. His reply
came back within a few minutes.

Do you still live in Queen's Park?

Marcella waited for the boys to come out of school. She didn't mind
that Thérèse had dumped Michel on her without warning. He was
charming, and good company for Hugo. He was beautiful like his
mother, with large eyes and silky blond hair. He wasn't ferocious
like Thérèse, but he was bouncy, tough and good humoured. Thérèse
and Luc had been at war all his life; now they had separated, and he
had been brought to London. He didn't seem crushed or unnerved
by the move. He had a wry personality.

The boys came rushing out. They bounced around Marcella.

They wandered across Queen's Park. Hugo and Michel kicked
a football between them. Marcella bought muffins and a takeaway
coffee and sat watching them play. It was late summer and the park
was full of dim green light, dreamy and dusty under the thick leaves.
Some local mothers joined her and they talked lazily while the kids
played. She thought about her dinner party. She would invite too
many, it would be chaotic, they would drink a lot and it wouldn't
matter if the duck smoked out the oven and set the fire alarm going.
She would let Hugo stay up with the adults. He could help her with
the cooking.

She made sure they stayed out as long as possible and when

they got in the boys were tired. She put on an audio book for them. Michel lay on his back on the rug, with his feet up against a chair. Hugo played dreamily with a plastic plane.

The phone rang. Thérèse said, 'I'm in the flat.'

'Have you got it?'

'It's gone. He's moved it, the fucker. He's hidden it.'

'Have you looked under the bed?'

'Under the bed? Are you joking, I've practically demolished the flat. I found some alien underwear. The pig.' She paused. 'God, someone's outside the door. Hang on.'

There was a bang and a burst of rapid French, Thérèse haranguing, a man replying. Another bang. Marcella listened. Thérèse was so bilingual she mixed up her English and French.

Marcella said, 'Hello? Thérèse?'

She came back on. 'Just the concierge.'

'He'll tell Luc you've been there.'

'Well, too bad. I'll be gone.'

'He must have stashed the painting somewhere else,' Marcella said. She glanced in at the boys. 'You'd better get out of there.'

'No, I'm sure it's here somewhere. He's not going to traipse around Paris with it. He's too lazy.'

'Well. The boys are fine,' Marcella said.

'Okay. I'll keep looking. I'll ring you.'

Marcella went into her room and switched on the computer. She looked at Richard Black's last message. She clicked on reply.

Yes. I still live in Queen's Park. This weekend I am looking after a little boy while his mother goes to Paris to steal an extremely valuable painting from her ex-husband's flat. She's in the flat right now, but he's hidden the painting. She's just been surprised by the concierge, but she's going to steal the thing anyway. If she can find it. Perhaps you could use this in a novel or story. Marcella

She went to the kitchen and started preparing food. The boys were still absorbed so she checked the computer again. He had replied.

Perhaps she misses him. She wants him to come raging after her to get it back.

Marcella dried her hands and sat down. She typed,

We can be pretty sure he will. She's already asked me if she can hide it at my house. I said, He'll think of that won't he? Since she and I are best friends. I'll have to deal with him breaking in here, after he's smashed his way into her place.

The reply came back: *Will he be murderous?*

She typed: *Undoubtedly.*

He replied: *I hope your husband owns some sort of firearm?*

She sat for a moment.

Then she typed: *My husband no longer lives with me.*

She got a strange, cold feeling. She stood up abruptly and rushed to the living room. She hugged Hugo hard and he pushed her away, ducking her kisses.

'Food in five minutes,' Marcella said loudly, and rushed into the kitchen. She poured herself a glass of wine and stood at the sink, looking at her reflection in the window.

She gave the boys their meal and then took them for a final airing in the park. The sky was all in flames and the air was warm, full of floating dust. They wandered home and she put them to bed and listened to their whispering and giggling until they fell silent.

Thérèse didn't call. Marcella texted her and called her mobile but got no answer. She went to bed and had a dream about *The Little Match Girl*. Winter dark. Lighted rooms behind glass. The wind in the streets. Sentimental wailing of a violin.

The next morning, Saturday, she took the boys to her gym. They swam in the pool while she went through her routine. Marcella's gym was one favoured by celebrities. On the bike next to her, Princess Diana's brother, the Earl Spencer, pedalled furiously, a terrific sneer on his face. Once, in the changing room, Marcella had listened to Stella McCartney having a furious conversation on the phone with

Paul McCartney. She'd said, 'She's taken the plane? Without asking? Dad, she can't do that! She texted you what? Dad, that is absolutely disgusting. You keep that for the lawyers.'

Now, pedalling on her bike, Marcella thought about the exchange between the McCartneys. It was something she could describe to Richard Black. She planned an e-mail while she and the sweating Spencer pedalled on, until he gave a grunt, climbed off and limped away, pausing delicately to free his underwear from his bulging Lycra pants.

Marcella was in the changing room when her phone rang.

Thérèse said, 'Marce? I've got it.'

'Where was it?'

'He'd slid it behind a bookcase. I found it this morning, after a whole night of wrecking the place. I've put it in its case, tidied up a bit and I'm on my way.'

'Oh. God. Well done. He's going to be furious though, isn't he?'

'But it's mine. He knows it's mine. He's just hanging on to it because his TV show's been cancelled and he wants money. Because he wants to make trouble about Michel. Now I've got it. No more argument. Voilà!'

Marcella laughed. 'You'd better get out of Paris.'

'I'm on the way. I'm in a cab. I'll ring you when I get to London. Bye.'

Marcella went to find the boys. They were trailing out of the changing room, their hair and T-shirts wet, their eyes bloodshot from the chlorine.

'Look at Michel's scar, Mummy,' Hugo said.

Michel showed her a thick jagged purple scar along his wrist and forearm.

Marcella turned his arm over gently. 'Ouch. When did you get that?'

Michel said, 'At half-term. I was locked in the bedroom and I couldn't stand it. So I smashed the window with my hand.'

'You were locked in? Was this when you were in Paris?'

'Oui. I smashed the glass and it cut my hand, and I had to go to hospital and stay all night.'

'It's such a brilliant scar,' Hugo said enviously.

'It is a brilliant scar,' Marcella agreed.

She started to form a series of questions. But she glanced at Hugo. His eyes were shining. She said nothing, put her arms around their shoulders and ushered them out.

Marcella turned on her computer and checked the messages. The inbox was empty. She scrolled down. She clicked on Send/Receive. Nothing.

There was time to fill in before she gave the boys their evening meal. She ran her hands through her hair, quickly tied it back and rushed downstairs. 'So. Boys,' she said, 'what do you want to do now?'

'The park.'

'Aren't you sick of the park?'

'We want to play football.'

'All right. Okay!'

She put a book in her bag and took money to buy a coffee.

They ran away to the edge of the park. Marcella tried to concentrate on her book, but it was no good. She shifted restlessly.

She glanced up to check on the boys, and saw a man walking between the trees. He was shortish, with a head of curly hair. He reached the path and began strolling casually past the children's playground.

Marcella got up, shading her eyes against the low sun. Was it? It was. It definitely was. Richard Black.

He walked along the edge of the playground and began to head towards the gate. Marcella started forward. No. Not that way. She hurried towards him. She called out to the boys, startling herself with the loudness of her voice. 'Boys. Ten more minutes!'

She pretended to be looking at the boys. In the corner of her eye she saw Richard Black start towards her.

'Hullo! Marcella?'

She said, 'Oh. God. It's you. Do you live around here?'

'I do. Quite near here. Well, Regent's Park actually.'

Marcella put her hand up to her mouth.

'Just passing,' he said. 'I can see you're laughing at me.'

'No, no,' she laughed. 'It's just funny to talk to you so soon, after we've been e-mailing.'

He gestured. 'Is that the boy? The one whose mother's off stealing the painting?'

'Yes, the blond one. The other one's mine. Hugo.'

'Shall we sit down? I've got this fantastic headache.'

They went to a park bench.

'How's she getting on in Paris?'

'She's found the painting. She's on her way back.'

He said gloomily, 'Cruz-Anne's been away for months. I think she's decided to go Peruvian.'

'Oh.'

'We had a prodigious fight on the phone. She's highly strung. Which is a euphemism for 'mad', of course. She's got a Peruvian chap she does field work with . . .'

'Field work?'

'Yes. Well. You can imagine.'

There was a silence.

He said, 'I liked the story about Dickens and Hans Christian Andersen.'

Marcella said, 'Well, you mention fights . . . One night Dickens had a fight with his wife, got out of bed at 2 a.m. and walked all the way from Tavistock House to Gad's Hill Place. That's thirty miles. It took him seven hours. He slept on his feet some of the way.'

'Seven hours!'

'There's something touching about it, isn't there? You can see him walking right out of London, all alone, through the hours.'

'Yes.'

Marcella said, 'I've been thinking. I have to take the boys home now and feed them. I wonder, would you like to come along? I could give you a glass of wine.'

It was a hot evening. They sat outside in the small back garden. The boys ate at the wooden table. The doorbell sounded.

Hugo and Michel ran to it before Marcella could get up. She heard Michel shouting, 'Maman!'

'Hellooo,' Thérèse called.

Richard Black scrambled up. 'The painting?'

'Helloo, I'm back, hello Michel little darling, little mouse.'

Thérèse swept into the kitchen, Michel hanging on to her arm.

'I've got it, I'm back, success! Helloo Marcella, mwa, and who's this, he looks just like Richard Black! It is Richard Black! Hello.'

There was a short silence. Richard Black beamed. Marcella poured Thérèse a glass of wine.

Thérèse clapped her hands. 'Well. Do you want to see it?'

'Yes, yes,' they said.

She brought in the painting and slid it out of its packing case. In the dim room the colours glowed.

'It's beautiful. What colours. Such blues and greens. It's lovely.'

Richard Black went close. 'Good God. Is it a Matisse?'

Thérèse raised her glass and they clinked.

'Cheers.'

'Good heavens,' Richard Black said.

They went out into the garden and sat at the table. Thérèse propped the painting on the bench just inside the door. 'Nice, eh?' She lit a cigarette and sat complacently smoking.

Michel leaned on his mother's arm. 'Maman, can we play with your lighter?'

'Of course, my darling. You and Hugo go and make a little fire.'

Hugo and Michel went close to the brick wall and found an old pot. They piled bits of paper into it and set them on fire. The sky was growing dark and the trees glowed in the last of the light.

They watched the two boys leaning over the fire, their eyes shining. Michel jumped back. 'It sizzled my hair. What a smell!'

Behind them, the painting made a window of colour. They turned to look at it as they talked. Richard Black said, 'Tell me the story, from when you brought your son here to when you got back with the painting.'

Thérèse blew a stream of smoke into the air. 'Bien sûr. But only if you'll write it down.'

'Of course.' He rubbed his hands together. 'One's pilot light is always on.'

Marcella leaned forward to pour more wine. The boys threw something big on the fire; the flames crackled and flared; paper flew off and whirled in the air, showering sparks.

Marcella watched the sky changing from grey to dark. The fire made shadows on the brick wall. How strange, almost alarming it was, to feel so happy.

GIVING UP
GERRY MCCULLOUGH

The afternoon sun blazed through the front room window.

I moved forward, and pulled the heavy curtain halfway across.

June. A beautiful day.

I used to love days like these.

Sitting out in the sun, on Portstewart beach, with the kids playing happily round us, and Kathy stretched out in her bathing costume, drying out after her quick dip.

Nearly twenty years ago.

Somehow, it wasn't the same, now.

The kids had grown up and gone, Kevin to Australia, Maggie (I must remember to call her Margaret) to Scotland, wee Dominic to Belfast. He was the nearest, but somehow I seemed to see less of him than any of the others.

The sun was still blinding me.

I twitched the curtain farther over, irritation in all my movements.

Instead of sitting down to watch the rest of the racing, I found myself gravitating to the kitchen, to the wall cupboard.

The bottle was empty.

I couldn't remember finishing it, but I suppose it wasn't the mice.

Now the struggle.

To buy more. Or to have the sense to cut back a bit.

*

It didn't take all that long.

I sighed, patted my pocket to check that my wallet was still there where it should be, opened the front door.

I had the key in my pocket as usual.

Okay. The off-licence was about a half mile walk.

Good for me, the walk, wasn't it? Better to be out taking exercise than sitting in the house all day.

Yes, of course.

The giro had come in the other day, so no problem there.

By habit, I had changed into my working boots before leaving the house, though why, I couldn't have told you. It was several years now since I'd needed them for working, since I'd been turfed out of my job.

I struck out across the grass behind my house. It was bright with daisies and buttercups, lit up by the sunshine, like sweet hopes for the future.

My feet in the thick working boots crushed them down as I walked.

Never saw any clover, these days. White and purple, there should be. Purple vetch, as well.

Halfway across the stretch of grass was the beginning of the pile for the bonfire. The kids started collecting early. When I was a youngster, they didn't start until July.

There were piles of good pallets, like they would use on the building sites. How they got hold of them, I didn't know. Nicked them, likely. Valuable stuff, not just rubbish for a bonfire.

I knew all about pallets. Spent most of my working life shifting them about with the fork-lift.

Until I lost my licence, and the job with it.

Maybe if I hadn't had that fight with the foreman, they might have given me some labouring work.

But he was a right git, deserved all the names I'd called him.

Ended up punching him in the face.

I grinned at the memory. Then wondered what was so funny about getting myself fired out of work.

A long time ago now.

Nothing to do with me if the kids nicked the pallets. Served the bosses right.

The off-licence was open.

'Morning, Hughie.'

'Morning, Charlie.'

The youngster behind the counter smiled at me. I counted him as a friend. He was always cheerful, happy to see me, I thought.

Of course, I was a pretty regular customer. He would need to look pleased.

I dismissed the thought.

'A bottle of your cheapest, Charlie,' I said.

'Whiskey, right? No problem, Hughie.'

He took the tenner, winked at me, and got the change.

'Beautiful weather we're having, Hughie. Reminds you of when you were my age, I bet? Right, Dad?'

'Yeah.'

'So you've told me many a time.'

I wasn't entirely sure how to take Charlie sometimes.

I grabbed the plastic bag and headed home again across the grass.

It was my evening for calling with Niall O'Hanlon and going to the Horseshoe Arms for a quick pint.

Niall gave me a funny look when he came to the door.

'Are you all right, Hughie?'

'Never better, Niall.'

I had tripped slightly over the step, but nobody would have noticed.

'Thing is, Hughie, I've got a friend here with me...'

'Sure, bring him along, Niall!' I said cheerfully. 'The more the merrier, right?'

'It's not a him, it's a her,' Niall said. He seemed a bit annoyed.

A good-looking wee red-haired woman appeared behind him in the doorway.

'What's up, Niall?'

Niall turned round and whispered to her.

Although I couldn't hear what he was saying, I heard her answer clear enough.

'Sure, there's no problem. We'll all go down the pub for a round or two. No need to stay late, eh?'

I saw her give Niall's arm a squeeze. Then he turned round and gave me a grin.

'Fair enough, Hughie. We'll all go. But Bridie and me won't be staying late, right?'

We headed off down the road.

The pub was in walking distance. Just as well. Neither Niall nor me had a licence now.

There was noise and music coming from the open door. It was going to be a good evening.

I took a good sideways look at this Bridie.

Quite a look of my Kathy, she had. Small, neat, cheerful, and the red hair. The way Kathy had looked, just before she ran off with her big American.

Four years ago, it must be. Just after wee Dominic moved up to Belfast.

I wondered suddenly if she'd been meaning to go for years. Just waited till the wee one had moved out and set up his own life.

It was a hard thought. I turned my mind from it.

'What'll you have, Bridie?' I asked. 'Half pint? And a pint for you, Niall, my old mate?'

I went off to the bar. Better get a whiskey for myself. Didn't do to change your tipple halfway. Best make it a treble, in fact.

I could feel Bridie's eyes on my back.

She fancied me, I could tell.

Sure, Niall was a good lad, but not one to get far with the women. He was my best friend, these days, I supposed.

Ever since that row with Peter McBride, a year or two ago.

Peter.

We'd been best mates since primary school.

What was it we'd fought about?

I couldn't even remember.

Maybe I could give him a ring sometime. See if we could make it up.

Meanwhile, there was Niall.

I wouldn't want to say anything against Niall. But, sure, he'd never had the gift of the gab, like me. And as for his looks, he was an ugly big critter, when all was said and done. Not one that the women would fancy.

I was coming up to fifty, okay, but I still had the pull.

I was in good form, that night, if I say it myself.

The two or three whiskeys in the afternoon had helped me. Or maybe it was four or five. Hard to keep track, sometimes.

'Well, Bridie,' I said jovially, 'it's not often I meet such a good-looking woman as yourself!'

She smiled.

Niall didn't seem so pleased, but he was always a bit of a sour one, come to think of it.

I ignored him, and went on talking to Bridie.

After a while, I got her up to dance.

She was a warm, cuddly bit of an armful. I pressed up close to her, enjoying myself.

Then Niall tapped me on the shoulder.

'My turn, Hughie.'

I was in two minds about letting him away with it. I was sure Bridie didn't want to stop. But, there, another fight mightn't be the best idea.

I went to sit down.

The room was swimming round a bit.

The heat, maybe, and the loud music.

Bridie and Niall came back to the table, and I pulled myself together.

I started to tell funny stories. For once I found myself remembering them. Some of them were a bit blue, but I didn't think Bridie was the type to mind.

I edged closer to her along the seat, and after a while I put my hand on her knee, under the table, right, so Niall wouldn't see. I gave her a wee squeeze.

Then Niall got her up to dance again.

I sat on.

After a while, things began to get blurred. The room seemed brighter, but farther away. It seemed to me that they had come back, and Bridie sat up close to me, put her arms round me, and began to kiss me. Her hands were all over me. She put her leg over my thigh, twisting round to face me, rubbing herself against me. I responded eagerly.

'Ah, Kathy, baby,' I muttered. Which one was it? It seemed as if it was both of them.

Someone was shaking my shoulder.

I swam up out of my dream, and heard voices in the distance.

Then they got more distinct.

'I'm sorry, Bridie.' It was Niall's voice. 'Sorry for letting you in for this. He used to be a decent mate.'

Then Bridie's voice. 'Sure, never worry, Niall, love. Dear help him, he's nothing to take seriously. Just a joke, so he is, nothing to worry about.'

I noticed that my head was on the table, resting on my arms.

I don't remember getting home, to tell you the truth. Niall must have helped me.

One thing I do remember, though. When we came out of the pub, there were people singing on the far side of the road. I wanted to stop and listen, but there was a drag on both my arms, and I went with it.

'*What a friend we have in Jesus,*' they were singing.

I remembered it from years ago. Kathy picked it to sing at our wedding.

There was something urging me to stop, to listen. But the hands on my arms were forcing me to totter on. There was no strength in me to resist them.

Next morning, when I woke up, I was lying on my sofa.

I didn't feel too good.

Kathy's chiming clock, striking, told me it was afternoon already.

I lay about until tea-time, then I made myself some baked beans on toast, and had a whiskey or two. After that I felt better.

I watched some television, had a few more drinks.

It helped me to forget the things I had heard when I came up out of my dream.

Which had been the dream, and which the reality? Bridie couldn't have really said those things, could she?

Bridie had liked me, I was sure of it.

So why would she say what she had said?

A joke. I was just a joke.

I must have dreamt it.

It would have been near half-ten when the phone rang.

I got to it just in time, tripping over the carpet where there was a bit of a rip, as I staggered over to the handset.

'Yeah?'

'Dad? Is that you?'

'Maggie? Is it yourself?'

'What? What? Dad, I can't make you out. Is that you?'

I pulled myself together.

'It's me, Maggie.'

'Oh, Dad, I need help. I need someone to talk to!'

'I'm here, Maggie.'

'It's wee Patrick, Dad. They say he's got leukaemia, Dad. Oh, Dad, what am I going to do? Mark and me are both so miserable. I need someone to talk to.'

I couldn't believe it. Wee Patrick, my only grandchild. What could I say to help her? I didn't know.

I began to talk feverishly.

'Maggie, it'll be all right. The doctors can do bloody miracles these days. If they've got it in time, they can make him better. I was watching a programme on TV the other night about it. Don't be crying, lass. Your Dad's here. I love you, wee Maggie....'

'What? What? Dad, I can't make you out. You're mumbling. What did you say?'

'Maggie, I love you... and I love wee Patrick...'

'Dad, you've been drinking!' Her voice sharpened with anger.

'Just a bit, girl.'

'I can't make out a word you're saying. Oh, Dad, can't you get a grip on yourself!'

'Maggie, I didn't mean to...'

Her voice grew even sharper. 'It's Margaret. Not Maggie. Margaret.'

'Sorry, Maggie.'

'You're useless, Dad. I needed you tonight, Dad. But you're no good. Just useless.'

The phone was slammed down at the other end.

I staggered back to the sofa.

It seemed as if there was nothing I could do. Nothing to help.

Next morning my head was sore.

I was still lying on the sofa. Hadn't made it to bed, last night.

What was I to do?

I didn't want to drink. Hair of the dog—yuk!

The idea revolted me.

Memories kept coming back.

Young Charlie laughing at me up his sleeve.

Niall looking angry. I suppose he didn't like the way I was getting off with his girl. Another friend on the way to being lost, was it?

Bridie calling me a joke.

But over and above all these, there was Maggie.

Of all my children, Maggie had always been the closest to me, maybe because she was a girl. I remembered her supporting me more than once when Kathy had been laying into me for the drinking.

What had I done?

Had I lost her for good?

And wee Patrick.

The song came back to me from last night.

'*What a friend we have in Jesus,*

All our sins and griefs to bear...'

I stood up. Made it into the kitchen.

Took the remains of the whiskey bottle from the cupboard, and poured it down the sink.

I felt better.

The day wore on.

About the middle of the afternoon, I thought I would phone Peter McBride.

'Are you there, Peter?'

'Yes, who is it?'

'It's me, Peter. Hughie O'Donnell.'

I could hear Peter at the other end draw his breath in sharply.

'What do you want?'

'Well, Peter...'

'What?'

'I just thought... You and me's been pals for a long time, Peter. It's a shame we never see each other these days…'

'Hughie, you know fine why we don't see each other. After that night, I told you I never wanted to have anything to do with you again!'

'Ah, Peter, if I spoke out of turn, I can only say I'm sorry…'

'Hughie, I put up with you and put up with you for long enough, but it was just too much in the end. After the things you said about me that night, I reckoned we'd be better apart. It was you raising your fist to me that finally did it, you know that rightly! I walked out before I ended up beating the hell out of you! Spoke out of turn, did you? That's one way of putting it. Ah, don't remind me! It's the drink does it, Hughie. Are you still drinking?'

I hesitated.

Do your friends despise, forsake you…?

'Maybe not, Peter. I'm thinking about it.'

'Well, when you're doing more than thinking about it, you can ring me. Till then, I don't want to hear from you.'

Another phone slammed down.

It was a glorious day. The sun was blazing in through the window again.

I headed for the kitchen. After the way Peter had spoken to me, I really needed a drink.

It was only when I reached the cupboard that I remembered pouring the remains of the bottle down the sink.

Great.

Okay, wait, it had been the right decision. If it wasn't there, I couldn't drink it.

I sat down again in front of the television, but after a few minutes I got up and began to wander round the room. I couldn't seem to settle.

I would be better out in the fresh air, I thought.

Maybe a short walk would be good for me.

But not to the off-licence, right? No sense in that.

Still and all, what harm did the occasional drink do, if it wasn't a matter of overdoing it?

Maybe if I just strolled up that direction, and made my mind up when I got there?

No harm in having a bottle available.

I didn't need to go overboard with it.

I could be a moderate drinker, for sure, like most people, if I just put my mind to it. It was the overdoing it that was the problem.

I patted my pocket to make sure that my wallet was there.

My key was in my pocket as usual.

I set out across the grass behind my house. It was bright with buttercups and daisies, lit up by the sun, like sweet hopes for the future.

My feet, in the heavy working boots, no longer any use to me, but still worn out of habit, crushed the flowers down as I went on walking.

ITALIAN LESSONS
GRACE FRENCH

It is a sunny morning in early October. Angel puts on her blue felt hat and taps the good luck coin wedged inside its brim. Clipping Betty's pearls around her neck, she goes into the sitting room to say goodbye to Martin. She kisses her husband on the top of his head, avoiding the bald patch and trying to ignore the smell of Sudocrem.

'Don't be long.' He doesn't lift his head from the *Racing Post*. 'And don't forget your helmet.'

'As if.'

Angel passes the hall mirror, her handbag in one hand and the cycling helmet in the other and, although she doesn't like what she sees, she smiles anyway. She gets her Raleigh bicycle from the garden shed and wheels it to the front gate. She climbs on board and tosses the cycling helmet into the lavender bush then pedals out onto the road. It is the first Saturday of the month, the day allocated to breaking rules.

She is meant to be going to Rafferty's organic butchers on Stanford Lane to buy Martin's lunch but when she reaches the bottom of the road Angel turns right towards Marble Hill. She pedals past what used to be O'Loughlin's fruit and vegetable shop, which now sells mobile phones. She zooms past the derelict cinema site with its silent crane, its boarded graffiti-sprayed doors and its canopy of sprouting weeds. Angel is heading in the opposite direction to Rafferty's butchers because she is not going there. She is going to meet Derek, a trip she has made every first Saturday morning of the month for nearly a year. Nestling in her handbag in the front basket of the bicycle is a freezer bag with the frozen fillet steaks that are Martin's monthly treat.

Angel reaches the bottom of Marble Hill and dismounts. She pushes the bicycle halfway up the hill, then stops. She always stops at this point, not just because she likes to look at the sea and the few fishing boats returning to the harbour, but because she can get a view of Derek's house. She cannot see it clearly at this distance but she knows that the red berries of his neatly clipped Cotoneasters will be gleaming in the autumn sunshine, the hanging flower pots will be swaying on his front porch and his brass door knocker sparkling clean. Today Angel lingers a bit longer than she normally would. She watches the sea and smells the faint whiff of a forbidden bonfire and feels sad. Perhaps it's the fact that winter will be here so soon. She climbs back on the bicycle, pedalling until she picks up enough speed to freewheel down the hill to Derek's front door. She fixes her hat and catches her breath before leaning the bicycle against the redbrick wall. The hall door opens.

'Morning, Mrs Finnegan. Come inside, I've got a surprise for you today.'

'Morning, Mr Reid.'

Angel hangs her coat and hat on the wooden hall stand and follows Derek into the study. A vase of white tulips sits on the desk, the flowers so perfect they could be plastic. When she sits down she puts her faux snakeskin handbag underneath the chair and removes her shoes.

'What's my surprise then, Derry?'

'Today, my dear Angel.' Derek smiles. 'Today we are going to Florence.'

Angel met Derek Reid in Rafferty's butcher's shop a year ago. She hadn't seen him since she was a young girl and at first she didn't recognise the old man with the sleek white hair and the crumpled navy cords. He was buying a pork chop and when the butcher handed him the piece of meat wrapped in its single sheet of greaseproof paper, Derek had started to cry. Loud gasping sobs filled the busy shop while in between he gulped to all and sundry how he had recently been left a widower.

'After thirty-five years!' he howled.

Angel forewent her place in the queue and took him next door to The Crazy Crumb. It took a pot of Earl Grey and a Danish pastry before she realised who he was, before she realised that this was the same Derek Reid who had broken her heart all those years ago, when she was barely twenty one. By this time he had calmed sufficiently to explain that he had just moved back into the neighbourhood, to a house not far from his childhood home. From the expression on his face, and the way the tears were beginning to well up once more, Angel felt that he had returned there to die.

'This is a beginning, Derry, not an ending.' She reached across the table and squeezed a thin, blue-veined hand. 'Regard this as a new chapter in your life.'

She didn't know why she had squeezed his hand and hoped he didn't get the wrong impression. Also, she had no idea why she had used those stupid words, new chapters and beginnings, she sounded like some New Age crazy woman when it was perfectly obvious that the poor man felt he had reached the end of his own particular road.

'I recognised you immediately.' He gripped her hand.

A few minutes' silence followed this obvious untruth and when Angel finally broke the silence, it was to tell Derek that she came to Rafferty's once a month.

'Yes, of course, I'd love to see you again,' she heard her voice saying.

'Same time same place next month, then?' He clutched the pork chop against his heart.

Angel didn't understand why she kept the meetings a secret from Martin. There was nothing to hide, just two old acquaintances meeting once a month for a cup of tea. Angel had never lied in her life before but she reasoned it was never too late to learn and after three meetings she became adventurous and ordered a cappuccino with cinnamon topping.

'I'd love to go to Italy. I've always wanted to speak Italian.' She spooned brown froth into her mouth.

'I can teach you Italian.' Derek reached across the table and touched her cheek.

Derek had worked in Milan for a year. It was a long time ago and his Italian was a bit rusty but he bought a set of Italian language CDs and a Nespresso coffee machine and so their monthly arrangement changed. Angel bought the steaks elsewhere and stored them in the freezer and she enjoyed the ridiculous subterfuge. She went to Marks and Spencer's and bought red and black lace underwear. She stored them in her night dress drawer and took them out on those Saturday mornings when she was meeting Derek. One day she planned to wear them.

Angel loved learning Italian. She would close her eyes as the liquid voice on Derek's CD player filled the study and Derek's coffee maker rumbled in the kitchen. Derek's house smelled of coffee and of open widows and for two marvellous hours every month Angel was able to forget about her life. She forgot about the boxes of Martin's medications on the coffee table, the faded chintz curtains and the grimy windows through which daylight oozed. She forgot about the smell of their poor old cat, a smell which no amount of lavender air freshener could camouflage.

'Come and sit beside me, Angel.' Derek pulls out a chair for her. 'You won't be able to see the computer from over there. I have it all set up for that trip you've always wanted to make and you don't even have to get on a plane.'

Angel sits beside Derek. She has never sat on this side of the desk before. She doesn't want to admit to him that she is afraid of his computer and she hopes he won't make her do something which will display this fear. Maybe, when she has mastered the Italian language, he can give her computer lessons. As his fingers fly over the keyboard she realises that she doesn't remember what he looked like all those years ago when he told her he preferred another girl to her, when she spent two days crying on her bed while her mother banged on her bedroom door, telling her there would be other boys. The funny thing is, she remembers exactly what her rival looked like, a wispy girl with hair the colour of dust.

'Look.' Derek points at a thumb-sized photo that has appeared on the screen. 'That's Florence, click on it and we're up and away.'

Angel puts on her reading glasses and takes the mouse from his hand. It feels warm and strangely intimate and when she nervously clicks on it Michelangelo's David fills the screen.

'Goodness. He's very big.'

Angel tries not to look too closely and hopes that the next image will be of a building or a square. She is annoyed by her embarrassment, as though she has never been married or given birth, and she hopes that Derek doesn't notice.

'Click again. Keep clicking on the arrows and I'll get the coffee and the Panforte.'

Angel clicks again and the Ponte Vecchio appears. It is night time and the bridge is brightly lit and filled with tourists and shoppers. She closes her eyes and imagines standing on the bridge wearing a red coat and matching red leather gloves and carrying one of those old-fashioned Chanel bags from the nineteen sixties. Suddenly Betty appears, her beloved childhood friend who died so long ago. They link arms and look down into the dark waters of the river Arno.

When Angel opens her eyes Florence has disappeared. She must have leaned forwards and pressed the keyboard because now there are many tiny pictures on the screen. She slides the mouse towards one marked 'holiday snaps'.

The first picture is of a beach. There are straw beach huts and golden sand and Derek is sprawled on a striped deck chair with a small boy on his knee. Derek is wearing a sun hat, his nose is red and he holds a bright blue drink with paper umbrellas. The boy looks about ten and is wearing a T-shirt with a picture of Bruce Springsteen. Angel remembers that Derek mentioned going to Thailand after his wife died but he never mentioned that he had so many young Thai friends. There are more shots of Derek's friends, and of Derek seated in a rickshaw, on the balcony of some hotel, or standing at a bar with a young girl with a bright face and a gap toothed smile. In the final photo he is alone in what appears to be a bedroom, except he is not on his own because the photographer's shadow falls across the bed and a pair of small sandals lies on the floor.

Derek comes into the study. He is carrying a loaded tray and singing 'La Donna Immobile'.

'How was Florence?' He puts the tray down.

The tray has coffee and steaming milk and that Italian cake that sticks to her teeth. Today he has added a single red rose in a glass stem.

'I don't know. I didn't stay very long. I went to Thailand instead.'

Angel looks at her feet. It is as if she is seeing them for the first time. They are swollen from the uncomfortable new shoes and the nail polish is chipped. When she was twenty-one she had tiny delicate feet.

'How on earth did you get to Thailand?'

Derek has sat down in the chair in which she usually sits. His tone is light but his eyes have narrowed and his eyelids are like the blinds in her spare bedroom, crumpled and beige.

Angel drops her head in shame. She has no idea why this has happened but it is as if all the shame she has ever felt has come to the surface, all the things she should have done, all the things she shouldn't have.

'I don't know how I got there, Derry, but I rather wish I hadn't.'

Angel gets her shoes and her bag and as she walks into the hall she notices that her bag is dripping blood. The freezer bag must have burst. She puts her bleeding bag onto the shiny polished surface of the wooden floor and puts on her hat and coat. When she goes out of the house she leaves the front door open.

She pushes her bicycle back up the hill and stops at the usual spot. She looks back but she doesn't wave at the tiny figure standing in Derek's doorway. When she gets home she puts her helmet and her bicycle into the shed and she opens the front door. She runs her right hand over the crack on the wooden surface of the hall table. Martin has been meaning to fix this crack for the last twenty years and she is glad that he hasn't.

Just then she hears Martin's voice. It is loud because he has the television on.

'Is that you, Angel?'

'Who else would it be?' Her voice is calm.

'I'm starved.'

Angel goes into the kitchen and takes out the frying pan. She chops three onions and tries not to cry. She fries the onions and the steaks and adds two eggs and when it is all cooked she puts it onto a plate. She carries it into the sitting room and plonks it onto Martin's lap.

'Can I at least have a knife and fork?'

Martin turns awkwardly in his wheelchair and the plate begins to slide.

'Use your fingers.'

OUR FELLOW CREATURES

GORAN PETROVIĆ

Translated from the Serbian by Peter Agnone

00:53

It must have been the middle of the night when the knocking roused him. His wife didn't even turn over. She was probably dreaming of somewhere far away. Once, in the past, he had sat beside her and watched her wriggling, taking the longest time to wake up, struggling to penetrate the dried membrane between two worlds, and like a newborn unwillingly opening her eyes on the here and now.

'Jacob, dear, if you only knew how far away I was,' she had said purringly, stretching herself; from beneath the blanket protruded her tiny feet.

'Isn't it a little silly to undertake such a long journey, knowing you'll only have to come back again?' he had asked.

Or had he wanted, being possessed of that very same desire, to justify himself, deceive himself?

00:59

The knocking was repeated. He got up, groped around for his felt slippers, fastened the top button of his striped pajamas, left the room, cautiously passed through the hall and, sighing deeply, not revealing his presence, stood right next to the front door.

The tentative knocking was repeated. He was unsure whether to peep out, afraid that the person on the other side would hear him raising the cover on the peephole, and then he would need to think of a way to get rid of him—when he discerned a broken, pleading, feeble voice: 'Is there anyone here?

'Is there anyone...

'Open up...

'For God's sake, open up...'

And though he didn't know why he was doing such a foolhardy thing—he pulled the gnashing deadbolt. Removed the tiny clasp of the steel security chain. Turned the heavy Wertheim lock and key, pressed down on the chromed door handle, and opened the door slightly...

The weak light from the apartment, mostly from the ten-odd blinking pilot lamps of the various electrical gadgets, was insufficient to dispel such deep darkness. Nonetheless, he very quickly saw, just two steps in front of him, a stooping old man, dressed only in a kind of knee-length collarless shirt, frayed and faded. On his feet he wore medium-high boots, with untied laces, too big for him by at least three sizes.

'At this hour?!' Jacob muttered through clenched teeth; not knowing how near the visitor's face was, he refrained from saying something ruder.

'Forgive me...' said the old man, lowering his head in shame.

01:07

'All right...' he said, wishing to cut short this senseless standing at the door; the cold night was hovering round his bare ankles. 'Is there some sort of trouble? You aren't ill, are you?'

'No,' sighed the silhouette in the shirt.

'Come on, what is it...?' asked Jacob.

'I'm, you know, I'm...'

'What?' Jacob asked more patiently. 'What's happened to you?'

'I'm lost!' said the old man, finally lifting his head. 'I came downstairs, I can't recall from where and why... I came downstairs and now I don't know how to go back...'

01:18

He wasn't sure he felt pity. Still, he couldn't just slam the door on him like that. After all, it was as if he'd seen him somewhere before. He was no doubt from the same building. Now he was already remembering that sunken chest, the pronounced collar bones, the slumping shoulders, the rather long, pure white, tangled hair, that somewhat teary gaze... Tomorrow he would surely reproach himself for not wanting to help a neighbour. And what's more, one well on in years.

He decided. Stepped out of the apartment. So as not to waken the tenants, considerately closed the door. Emboldened, the darkness rushed from a hundred corners, gnawing down to ghostly shadows the otherwise meagre semblances of light. He searched for the light switch, but it only clicked ominously. The stairwell lighting didn't work; for years the residents had been unable to agree among themselves about replacing the burnt-out automatic device. The only thing you could rely on was the light shaft, if a space that has for decades been crammed with junk can be called that. Junk apparently older than the building itself, which had seemingly been built around it.

'Don't you worry, now,' he said slowly. 'What floor do you live on?'

'I told you... I don't remember...' replied the old man.

'And what's your name?'

'No, I don't know that either, my good man... It's as though I've never had my own name...' said the lost one, almost beginning to sob. 'Forgive me...'

01:36

A draught was coming in from somewhere. It carried with it the dank smell of the basement, the stench of poorly washed vats for sauerkraut, the stale odour of tobacco smoke and the preparing of evening meals. Jacob wanted to go back for his vest. But that would only prolong this unpleasantness. He remembered who lived on the lower floors, and who on the floors above his apartment. He didn't know them by name. The question was whether he had ever made the acquaintance of any of those people. He probably had, but, of course, a very long time ago. Faces. Yes, he remembered some of their faces. He had greeted them, when there hadn't been anyone else around, in the hallway of the building. One of them, no doubt, belonged to this unfortunate man. He took him under the arm and set out at random…

They climbed slowly. His bedroom slippers made a slapping noise. The old man's untied boots caught on the steps. The darkness was filled with a muffled knocking.

'You have no keys. That means the door is open…' he said, just in order to say something.

01:51

He didn't know why, but they didn't stop on the next floor. The old man was breathing hard. Maybe sighing. Jacob wondered whether he was hunched over with age or whether birth had loaded that sad burden upon his back. Now it was clear to him that he felt compassion. But why did the old man have to knock precisely on his door? There were more than a hundred apartments in the building. How many floors there were, he didn't know. He lived on the ninth. Those above him didn't interest him. But, he suspected, the building was tall, too tall. Several times they had added on to it. A contemporary Tower of Babel. At first they had supposedly humbly sought the agreement of the tenants, and afterwards no one had even bothered to ask them. There had been new mailboxes, crisscrossing metal scaffolds, people wearing glasses with levels and plans on transparent blue paper, winches and cranes, the cursing of craftsmen, stacks of boards for siding, the shouts of carpenters and plumbers, lumps and lumps of plaster, pipes of various diameters, iron in the shape of horseshoes and nails, sawdust, bundles of welding rods, dislodged nests, feathers flying everywhere, dead birds, cauldrons of bubbling tar; new trucks kept arriving, weighted down with metal frameworks, cinder blocks and freshly poured, prefabricated sections of interior walls…

His companion said nothing. He just breathed loudly. As if he were made entirely of something that rustled…

The glass was missing from one of the frames of the light shaft. For a moment Jacob left the old man's side. He stuck his head through and looked all around. What a pity. Like a rotted oak. Instead of white pith, only scattered flickers of light. At the bottom a heap of everything, of all sorts of things.

02:15

Time was passing. Irretrievably draining away, drop by drop. One should have been resting. And not climbing in the dark with this unfortunate man, trudging aimlessly upstairs, only to stumble on muddy doormats, empty wine bottles, boxes, crates, ruined stoves, broken down love-seats and other junk that had been brought out onto the landings. Finally, did he know where they were going? Was it possible this unlucky fellow had no family of his own?

'Ha-dži-ta-na-si-je-vić,' he said, reading out the inscription on the brass nameplate.

The old man shrugged his shoulders.

'Danilo Al. Vidaković, certified and sworn court interpreter?' he barely managed to read on the next door.

The old man shook his head.

'Maržik?'

'Avramović? Zorka and Svetozar?'

'Klašnja? Civil servant?'

'Sidor Isidorovich?'

'Mrsać?'

'Šojka?'

'It is with grief and sadness that we announce to our relations and friends that on...'

'Trajan—Trajče Trajkoski?'

'Zečina?'

'Jovan Forcan, retired?'

'Milin? Hydrological engineer?'

'Ljubisavić, one long ring? Dinić, two short rings?'

'Ostraćanin?'

'Goluban Ćuk?'

'187?'

'188?'

'Vavan?'

'Petrović?'

'Hrane Tomova Rakočević?'

'Vivot, Justina, widow?'

'Sealed on the basis of Decision No. 73829 / 1997 by the investigating officers of the Interior Ministry?'

'Bumbarašević?'

'Perušina?'

'Gracijela Savčić-Savčić, Leading Lady of drama of the National Theatre?'

'Rajče?'

'204?'

'T. Kastelc? Pilot?'

'*Floor Area*, real estate agency, purchase, sale and exchange; brokerage, fully legally guaranteed?'

'Rečević?'

'Ilić-Uzeirbegović-Horvat?'
First names. Last names. Professions.
First names. Last names.
First names.
Nothing.

02:49

They sat on bundles of old daily newspapers to rest. As much as he was able, he discerned line by line of the old man's face. Although in his eyebrows he didn't have a single one of those wild hairs, the whites of his eyes were troubled, as if for a century and more they had kept watch over a vast sea of misfortune and grief. Further and further from his watery eyes, across his brow, down his cheeks and around his lips, the wrinkles had apparently not come from old age, but from a constant, painful spasm. And when he raised his right hand and slowly ran his long fingers through his hair, it seemed that the skin on the back of it was young, spotless, smooth. Why had he been wary for so long, and now so quick to believe a sorrowful stranger? And what kind of overly long sleeves were those? Weren't the shirts from sanatoriums for the insane similar to this one? Who was this odd fellow? What did he really want?

'Who are you?' Jacob nearly shouted.

The man shrunk, hunched over even more at the question.

'Do you hear me? Who are you? Who? Answer me!' Jacob seized him by the shoulder.

'Your fellow creature, for goodness' sake... your fellow creature...' repeated the lost one, as though his words were carried through the night on an echo, a mournful lament.

03:15

They went on. There were no longer any signs to indicate the floor. Judging by the rarefaction of the basement dankness, they must have gone quite far. Or maybe the benumbed human senses had been deceived, interpreting circling around as moving forward. Nothing had changed. Through the porous apartment doors came every sound imaginable:

...the nightmarish raving, gasping and wheezing of sleepers...

...the deep sighing and walking to and fro of insomniacs...

...the bitter family quarrels...

...the futile ringing of telephones...

...the crying of awakened children, their nappies wet...

...the desperate scratching of claws and the sniffing of shut-in, maddened dogs...

...the sounding out of lessons by students...

...the muffled hissing of televisions...

...one hundred, two hundred, two hundred and fifty, three hundred, three hundred and ten, three hundred and twenty—the recounting of savings put away for a rainy day...

...the interweaving waves of unbelievably distant foreign radio stations...

...the embellished, adorned telling of everyday stories...

...the striving and endeavouring of late-arrived lovers...

...the flushing of toilets...

The signs and inscriptions on the walls as well, senselessly similar.

The change was occurring only somewhere within Jacob. With each step or floor he climbed, he recognised an ever greater closeness. He could not explain it, but he suspected, was almost sure—that without his hunched-over companion—*he* would be the one who felt lost.

03:41

From above was heard the turning of a lock. After it, voices. And then a light began to move about. The blinding beam of a flashlight caught them on the landing. The person pointing it could not be seen.

'Where are you going?' Jacob made out, after which the newcomers whispered to each other for quite a while.

'Up...' he began to say, blinking, and then fell silent when he remembered what time of night it was, what he was wearing and how the man next to him was dressed.

The whispering behind the beam of light once more ended with a question:

'Are you looking for something? You're not lost, are you?'

Now already accustomed to the glaring light, Jacob turned to the man beside him. All contracted, shrunken in his long shirt, his hands crossed on his lower stomach, the fellow creature was breathing heavily and staring fearfully, like a hunted beast.

'No, we know where we're going!' Jacob answered as decisively as he could, observing the fear in his companion's eyes turn into gratitude.

'You see, they're some kind of vagrants! Homeless people; that entrance door should be locked...' one voice clearly stood out from the whispers.

'Shit, I know the hunchback from somewhere,' said the second voice, more loudly.

'Come on, forget them, we'll be late! Street people. And, you two, don't let us find you here when we get back!'

As the newcomers were passing them, they didn't turn aside the light beam. For some time they could be heard descending to the lower floors, and then everything became quiet again.

04:12

They went arm in arm. Jacob, saying nothing. The man, silent.

Neither of them spoke even when Jacob stumbled and cut himself on a shard of glass. Blood filled his palm, dripped between his fingers, at regular intervals marked their path. As though he himself were enduring the pain, his companion compressed the same spot on his own hand. The flow of blood stopped. The injury healed; before long the spot of the wound could not even be distinguished. If there hadn't been dark traces on the sleeve of his pyjamas, Jacob could have sworn that it had all been an illusion.

'Thanks,' he said, turning.

The outline with the white hair said sadly:

'It's nothing.'

04:34

The upper air must have been intoxicating. Unaccustomed to the freshness, Jacob felt dizzy. It was of no use even when he half unbuttoned his pyjamas. He stumbled more and more often, and felt less and less sure of himself. In the end it turned out that the other man was leading *him*, and not the other way around.

He collected himself only when his companion halted. He slowly bent down, picked up some kind of leaf, broke it and then twirled it in his fingertips. The pungent odour roused his strength.

'A lemon tree, here?' asked Jacob, amazed.

'A lemon tree, Jacob. We're probably not far…'

Jacob? Someone had long ago removed the nameplate from the door to his home. Or maybe he himself had done that. Only the number of the apartment remained. And he couldn't recall if more recently he had told anyone his name…

The floors followed one after another. Time somewhere surely meant something to someone, but it was as if they were exceptions.

05:11

Thus did they find themselves in front of a forced, wide open door. Beside the broken doorframe was a flowerpot of oleanders. Next to it another—with a small lemon tree. The wind gently stroked its leaves.

The passage looked out onto the sky. It was the very top of the building. An exit onto the unfinished roof. Abandoned scaffolding, the framing and joints, unused chimneys, reels of wire, scattered panelling, joists, a rusty saw and a coarse sieve for sand, the iron sinews of support columns, rotten ropes, antennae, antennae, antennae, a cauldron of dried tar...

Although narrowed at the bottom, although cramped by the building, the skylight here branched out into stars. Above, in the farthest forked twigs, the dawn began to bud. Nighttime is so: the dawn will advance, yet it will still be dark.

The companion removed his oversized boots and said:

'Farewell... And thanks... Now I remember everything.'

He smiled vaguely. He stooped as he passed through the doorway, then straightened up as he walked, shed his hair, and removed the shirt from his shoulders and back and became naked. Somewhere at the limit of Jacob's vision the rustling breaths became the rustle of feathers, that hump on the old man's back spread into a pair of large wings.

Jacob didn't want to go outside. He didn't want from such a height to see how far below the night was. Returning, going back downstairs, into the entrails of the building, he repeated:

'Don't get lost, don't get lost...'

Or these were the words of the fellow creature, echoing deep within him.

THE GRIND
DÓNAL MOLONEY

Buying the dairy products is looking like a bad bet, the sun having plenty of force left in it. Among other things, Brian has two litres of milk and eight yoghurts in his rucksack. He is sweating from his rush to get to the supermarket before it closed. His fleece-lined jacket and the weight of the groceries on his back aren't helping either.

On both sides of the street at improvised intervals are scrawny cherry trees, some of which are blossoming. People who worked late are coming home; others are leaving to pay visits, pursue hobbies or start night shifts. Cars, SUVs and vans jerk in and out of drives. There are children everywhere, running and cycling and generally squeezing fun out of this first sunny evening of the spring.

Brian stops in front of a house and checks his watch. Having found the house without any problems, he is a little early. He decides to go up and ring the bell anyway. While waiting, he consults his memory for the two names. Any anticipation he might have felt has been wrung out by tiredness.

The door is opened by a tallish woman, about thirty years old, with a tense face and shoulder-length stringy black hair. She is wearing a blue trouser suit, the jacket open over a cream blouse.

'Mr Delaney?'

'Brian. Call me Brian. You must be Helen.'

'That's right. Come in.'

She leads him through the hall into a steamy, cluttered kitchen, which smells of garlic and basil. On a dish rack, suds creep down the sides of two plates and a colander.

'Glorious evening,' she says, followed by an ironic snort which makes Brian swallow the 'Gorgeous!' his lips were framing in reply.

'You're a bit early. He's upstairs reading and he'll bite my head off if I disturb him.'

'That's fine. I'll look over my notes for the few minutes. Will it be here or...?'

'In there, I suppose is best.' She gestures behind her with the back of her head.

She brings him through the sitting room into the dining room, the two small rooms divided by a plywood sliding door, which she pulls across behind them.

'Can I take your jacket?'

'No, no need, thank you, I can just hang it over the chair here. If that's all right?'

Helen nods.

He sits down at the table and takes pens—one blue, one red—and a spiral-bound notepad out of his briefcase. The table is covered by a sky-blue tablecloth with a pattern of sheaves of golden wheat. There are four small lace doilies at each end of the table and a large one in the centre, on top of which sits a glass fruit bowl filled with apples, oranges and grapes. The apples and grapes are wrinkled, and a bluebottle vibrates on an orange. He wants to move the bowl and the doilies, but he can still feel her presence behind him.

'You said on the phone he was intermediate level, right?'

Actually, it was he who had used the word 'intermediate'.

'Roughly, yeah. You'll see for yourself.'

He feels the irritation in her voice, that she doesn't really know what an intermediate level of French is.

'His main problem's speaking,' she says, then adds pointedly, 'Oral.'

Then there is a thoughtful pause before her shoulders drop,

her face loosens up and she continues in a more open tone, 'He's got speech difficulties in general. Because of his face, what I told you on the phone. In English you can understand him perfectly once you get used to his voice a little. In French, obviously, it'll be tougher, but with practice and patience'—here the sharpness returns momentarily to her voice—'no doubt he'll be able to speak clearly in no time. He loves French, everything about France, wants to read his books in the original and be able to chat in French.'

'Sounds like a perfect student!'

He is used to overanxious questions from parents and adult students about French pronunciation. He has a good, fun system for practising it, using a little applied phonetics. He is explaining this to Helen when springs squeak upstairs. Then comes a clap like a slim paperback being dropped on a bedside table.

'Just don't panic if you don't understand him right away. His mouth is pretty bad.'

She gives him an insistent, challenging look.

Right, so he has a deformity: got it. It's the twenty-first century, I'm a professional. Trust me, it's grand.

'Has he ever seen a speech therapist?'

'Yeah, and it worked wonders. But there are physical impediments that, you know, set a limit, but, as I said, if you attune'—she gives the word 'attune' a sharp emphasis as if to say, *Yes, you heard me right, Mr Teacher*—'your ears, you'll understand every syllable. He's actually a stickler for pronunciation, often corrects me.'

'Hope he won't have to correct me!'

Helen doesn't laugh. She turns away to face the window and taps her clogs in slow alternation on the scruffy carpet. Why wasn't she calling him? He looks up at the round plastic clock on the wall. It's five past. He wonders what their relationship is. She said on the phone that he was twenty-five. Was she his sister? Were the parents still alive? Was this the family home? Or was she a housemate? His girlfriend? He is about to ask when he hears footsteps on the stairs.

'I'll leave ye to it.'

She goes to the door giving on to the hall. At the threshold, she stops and turns.

'Okay if we settle up later?'

'Fine, yeah.'

He is seated with his back to the door, his palms pressed on the table, ready to stand up to shake hands with his new student. There is a break in the two sets of footsteps as the two of them presumably exchange a look and maybe a gesture, then a shadow in the doorway. He rises and turns, a chirpy 'Bonsoir Jonathan, comment allez-vous?' on his lips. It dies there. There is an instant where his personality is wiped, all the defences of acquired behaviour breached. He manages a crooked, stupid smile (none of the ones in his repertoire) and holds out his hand. As Jonathan reaches forward to take it, Brian feels a kind of intimidation he has not known since he was a small boy in the presence of a tall uncle with a booming voice. Then Jonathan's hand is limply there in the sweat of his, the shake for Brian less a physical contact than a tactile hallucination.

As Jonathan takes the seat to his left, Brian falls back into his chair and glances over at him, deploying what is intended to be one of his stock classroom looks conveying kindness and competence. But his face does not obey, and lights instead on an expression of uncertain stupidity.

Jonathan looks over expectantly. Brian gazes down at the doily in front of him on the table and fiddles with his wedding ring, twisting it back and forth, what he saw still being processed in his inner eye: the mass of deformity on the lower face, centred on the mouth. The lips were a massive spread, encroaching the nose and chin and extending way into the cheeks. They were a livid red recalling weals and no skin sealed them, just tough flesh and sores. The gums were swollen and extremely wide, the teeth in them appearing tiny and sharp by contrast. The mouth as a whole was all flesh, exposure. It didn't seem to close fully, and the sound of panting came heavily through it. Brian thinks of burns, even a Chelsea smile, but these leave neater, more clearly delimited damage (in the case of burns, the trace of a trajectory, however messy). This was organic, heaving. And then there were the eyes as seen by him in the first unprotected moment, his perception of them distorted by the shock of the face framing them. The eyes in that first glance surely only contained the normal emotions on meeting someone new: curiosity, apprehension, plus whatever the young man's personality wanted them to convey, maybe confidence or wit or friendliness. But what Brian perceived in that flash of encounter was outrage, the outrage of intelligent, expressive irises in the shiny white of eyeballs fixed perversely to this face with the grossly deformed mouth. And not only outrage. He also perceived a shrill undefined plea, asking for much more than he was capable of giving. Just like the face itself was more than he was capable of taking in.

Brian decides to skip the preliminary chat in French to get an initial idea of the student's level. He doesn't trust his hands to be able to flick through to the right page on his notepad, so he flips it open on a blank page near the end. From behind the sliding door comes the sudden blare of a television, then the sound of the volume plummeting and a shallow cough.

'Well, nice to meet you, Jonathan. To start, I'll ask you a few general questions about your past experience of French, what you want from the grinds, that kind of thing. Did you do French in school?'

He forces himself to lift his eyes to Jonathan's face, but they flutter over it without really looking.

As Jonathan moves his mouth there's the sound of a sharp chomp, then the words, which are accompanied by a low hissing. The taut jaws struggle with the unwieldy flesh. 'I didn't...' is all Brian catches from the first sentence. When he misses the start of the second he panics and gives up trying to interpret. It is the same defensive instinct that kicks in when three or four boys in school are clamouring to tell him something.

When Jonathan has finished, Brian asks, 'And why do you want to have lessons now?' and turns his head to the left so that his marginally better right ear is in the direct flow of sound. 'Mainly because… understand… interested more in… there? where?… laity? And I'm… heaviness?… brother?… language.' But this improvement in how much he understands is as far as Brian gets. He works his way through the usual questions, pretends to take notes on the answers and doesn't grasp the substance of any statement. He has the feeling that he should be able to understand, that the fault is his; it is as if there is a little devil inside his head intercepting the key words and eating them up before they reach the brain. Every time he looks Jonathan in the face his eyes hop dizzily over the surface or else land on some feature (like the tongue lolling tinily in the relative hugeness of the mouth) that disturbs him. Every time he makes a determined effort at concentration he feels as if he is drifting dangerously far outside himself in pure attentiveness; that if he puts more of himself into listening, even more will be demanded of him.

Then Jonathan finishes an answer with rising intonation. 'Sorry, didn't catch that last part.' Jonathan repeats the question; Brian's devil eats up the meat of it. The bluebottle lands on one of Brian's knuckles and he shakes it off. 'Sorry again, what was the question?' There is frustration in Jonathan's voice as he asks the question for the third time. And a pleading, behind which Brian obscurely senses a threat. But again he doesn't understand what is asked. 'Generally speaking, yes, though not necessarily.' He nods at Jonathan and directs his eyes at him. Jonathan doesn't say anything, but Brian imagines him groaning inside.

Brian looks over at the clock: only twenty past. He is hot, and his ankles itch under his woolly socks. He doesn't know what to do next. Usually with new students he would spend the bulk of the first grind doing conversation and finish up with a pronunciation exercise or a short reading comprehension they would then discuss. Now, however, he wants to avoid anything which would put him in a position of listening and not understanding.

Just as he is about to excuse himself to go to the toilet he hears a floorboard creak in the hall. Helen listening in mistrustfully, he thinks. The room has been silent for a good half minute now as he pretends to look over his notes. He can't think straight. The thought of Helen behind the hall door oppresses him. He has to get out— Helen would have to scurry off.

'Very good. Before we go on, I have to go to the loo. Is there one upstairs?'

Jonathan nods, and Brian stands up, turns and strides to the door. Jonathan says something he doesn't catch, so he just mumbles 'Right, thanks.' Helen isn't in the hall. He resists the compulsion to let his face relax and express his anguish, as he suspects she may be spying on him from behind the kitchen door or over the bannister. The door on the landing is ajar and the corner of a fluffy pink rug juts out underneath it. He enters, and as soon as the door shuts behind him he mouths a silent scream. It is so violent his jaws seize. Pain surges around the lower half of his face and his eyes wear a look of scandalised victimhood. He rubs his jaws with the index and middle fingers of either hand, slowly closing his mouth. 'Ambush,' he thinks, 'an ambush is what this is.' Looking in the mirror, he is too agitated to bring his reflection properly into focus. Every object in his field of vision rocks and blurs. He sits down on the toilet seat and puts his head in his hands, the balls of his palms pressed against his eyelids.

It feels good to have his eyes closed and to massage his eyeballs. His lashes rustle pleasantly. No images burden his tired inner eye. Tired, that was it—'I'm so tired. If I wasn't so tired,' he whispers. Well-ordered thoughts come to him. He decides to give up on any notion of giving a good lesson and just get through it as best he can. A reading comprehension might be good, but there was the risk of Jonathan asking questions or discussing the text. Anyway, he still hasn't formed an idea of what his level is. He will spend the rest of the lesson running through verb tenses. That way he can do all the talking and will only have to look up from time to time.

He looks at his watch: twenty-five past. He stands up but feels dizzy and sits back down, retaking his previous pose. Every time he checks his watch time has moved slower than he expected. He stays sitting for two further, stolen minutes, time trailing with the fullness of transgression, then gets up to go back down to the lesson. But as he reaches for the door handle he hears footsteps coming up the stairs. He reckons this is Helen's way of telling him to hurry up. The footsteps stop without him having heard a door opening. He stands still for a full minute, pained and resentful, before he hears the steps again, this time going back downstairs. He leaves the bathroom and is already on the stairs when he realises he hasn't flushed the toilet or run the tap. He hesitates a moment but then presses on, marches into the room and throws a smile over in Jonathan's direction. Taking out his grammar book, he talks about how good it is and assures Jonathan that he will photocopy the relevant pages when using it in the future. He sounds authoritative and professional, but there is also a harshness in how he speaks. He tries to modulate the tone of his voice, but fails. His whole personality, all its fine nuances, is reduced to depressingly clunky choices, and here he chooses not to risk lapsing into panic, even if it means his voice is tinged with nastiness. Having finished praising the book, he tells Jonathan—and here there's a note of challenge in his voice—they are going to do verb revision, starting at the beginning with the *présent*.

For the final thirty minutes or so he talks at Jonathan, rarely looking up from his book. In his classroom, of course, he sometimes has to speak to the teenagers for long stretches at a time, though he avoids it as much as possible. For example, by breaking up his long explanation with questions to check comprehension. Or by trying to get a discussion going. But to speak to an adult continuously for half an hour—he feels the shame in this.

At one minute past the hour he gets up and packs away his stuff while waffling about his plans for the next lesson. Helen comes in carrying a purse. She asks him a few questions about Jonathan's ability. Brian makes up the answers, speaking rapidly and confidently in generalisations, not looking over at Jonathan. Helen does, though, gauging the truth of Brian's words in the face she is able to read intimately. Then she plucks out the thirty euros, which Brian takes from her with an odd, uncharacteristic little snatch. He tosses a goodbye at Jonathan and walks past Helen out of the room and to the front door, which he opens himself. He steps out and only turns to say goodbye to Helen when he is at the end of the drive. He flashes a smile at her and delivers a breezy 'See you next week,' then strides off listening out for the door's slam, and echo.

PROUD OF YOU NO MATTER WHAT
BENJAMIN ARDA DOTY

These hard economic times, barks an agitated male voice from one of
the many propped televisions over the loose congregation of sitting
and standing people en route some place. An airport janitor, spine
curved over like a twisted branch, in green pants and button-down
brown shirt, crumples a discarded magazine insert with latex-
gloved hands. *Come and go,* continues the voice. Pale beefy hands
with fingers thick as sausages reach into a bag of potato chips. Foil
crackles. *All made from scratch,* says a gentler voice. The ungreased
wheels of a rolling carry-on squeak like the rusted chains of a swing
set creaking under too much weight. *Jobs that pay six-figure salaries.*
The waft of poor sanitation escapes from the restrooms. Voices
mumble like false prophets from minarets and pulpits over a deaf
and blind audience. CNBC. CNN. Headline News. A power-push
dolly commanded by a government worker starts up like an aircraft
engine. *How bout that game last night.* A woman knits an ugly scarf
of oranges, pinks and blues under a miniature billboard that makes
a businessman look like a demigod. A two-hundred-page book on
what to think in small print rests on a lap still dirty with crumbs.
A silver-haired woman with skin sleeked like an eel's strums an
electric harp for guests who look even stranger than her. *Reflections*
is the title of the new album she's trying to sell. The carpet muffles
the sounds of a hundred soles. *Do not accept any items from unknown
persons.* Baby fat with a tuff of blond cries in a sky-blue blanket. *Do*

not leave your baggage unattended. Scorpion in a bottle of poison. *Please report any suspicious persons or unattended baggage to airport services immediately.* Keys and coins jangle in pockets. Behind glass, items prohibited and restricted by US Customs and Border Protection. *The US threat level is high, or Orange.* A well-dressed man ruffles his newspaper open. Smells like French fries. I sit with my back to no one, as I would in any potentially dangerous situation. Every sound, every patch of misplaced colour, every impending threat. This isn't combat anymore, but I can never tell what's over my shoulder.

One moment you're waiting at Chicago's O'Hare to go to San Francisco International and the next you're not.

The soldiers in their desert camouflage in the terminal look so young. The young soldier sitting in the lounge before my gate is quiet, aware that everyone watches him, as if he was a crucifix raised by a master of ceremonies to silence unruly children. Besides his pride, which is only acute when others watch him with shame and awe, he has his backpack and flak jacket. It is this jacket that makes the people thankful it's not their own bodies they have to protect from slugs and shrapnel. The young soldier boards business class. It is one of the perks that come with the jacket. *The crew would like to thank those on board, particularly the members and veterans of the Armed Forces choosing to fly with us today.* Several hands clap for the young soldier. Only several.

It's not me in those boots anymore. My seat is several rows behind, my ticket paid for by my father, my discharge other than honourable.

Quiet down, I tell myself.

I met my father outside Chicago's VA hospital, where I had been sent for PTSD and an impending court martial two months earlier, and we went to a roadside diner. He talked and I watched the steam off my coffee rising like mist off a lake on a cold morning.

'There are two ways to forget,' said my father, chewing his food.

'You can get Alzheimer's or die.'

I watched my father's lips. His upper lip was lazy. His lower lip revealed a row of crooked and yellowing teeth and strong gums.

'A refill?' asked the waitress.

'Please,' I said.

'I seen it many times,' said my father. 'You just live with it like another part of you.'

The nametag on the waitress's yellow-and-black striped blouse said 'Regina.' Her face was like that of a clown under the make-up, breaking apart behind aging skin.

'Thanks, Regina.'

The man across from me, my father, was the picture of myself in twenty-eight years. This was where I had to focus.

'Are you going to run?' said my father. 'Right here, right now? It wouldn't do any good if you did. You can't run from it any more than you can, say, dig a hole to China. I know what they say about the VA. Are they treating you well?'

'Yes. When does your plane leave?'

'Tomorrow.'

Most silences follow seven minutes of conversation. Our silence came after less than a minute. In less than two years, my father had aged ten. Time has a way of lunging forward when you think it's creeping. He was wearing a silver watch with a dial almost as thick as his wrist. It had a compass and digital box in military time, a gift from my stepmother. My father's hands, small and thick, were old and covered with liverspots. On his arm was the tattoo of his old company and the years 1967 and 1968 under it, a time he had talked about once. My father didn't look like the man who kept a shotgun under the front seat of the Dodge in case he had to one day put the muzzle up to his chin.

The coffee was black. My father looked out the unclean window in the direction of the highway. Two men and a younger boy slipped out of a king cab in camouflage one week into the hunting season.

'You served your country,' he said.

The coffee was still hot. I blew away the steam off its surface before taking a sip.

I looked out the window again at the cars and trucks driving across America, distances close and far.

'Son,' said my father.

'More coffee?' asked Regina.

'Yes.'

We were almost at the end of 2007. There were five individuals sitting behind us and three ahead of us. Two behind the counter besides Regina. There were four cars in the parking lot. Every once in a while I was distracted by the shuffling of the five civilians behind us. There was an urgency to always know who was close enough to be a threat. That's why malls were terrible places. You never knew. It was habit. In the old place, your attention couldn't lapse once. An insurgent with a weapon could appear from anywhere. An IED could explode at any moment.

Regina poured the coffee. I blew across its scalding surface again. I put the coffee down. My father watched me. My eyes closed.

'Dad, there's something very wrong with me,' I said, trying to keep my voice level. I was seeking my father's sympathy.

'We're proud of you no matter what,' he said, glancing down at his half-finished breakfast.

The temperature was 98 degrees, but would probably reach 110 by 14.00 hours. Dust blew across the landscape and covered everything. I hadn't seen a part of the country that wasn't like this. We'd been patrolling for eight hours in a town northeast of Baghdad where an IED had turned an APC with the four-man crew inside out. A car left in the middle of the street blocked our path. The sun made it impossible to look far above the horizon. Gunfire started coming in from several directions. There were civilians in the area. I was an SPC First Class by then in the 4th. One of the privates had taken metal in his shoulder. The civilians scattered. We radioed. We were part of a convoy of two APCs. The wounded private, my friend, screamed. Another person in my squad let loose the .50 cal. I got out of the APC to take up our flank with lethal fire. The sun blinded my line of sight, but I could see feet. It was him or me. I squeezed the trigger on my M4.

But the gun jammed and nothing happened. He ran away behind a building. Maybe he was thirteen or fourteen. I had almost killed a kid.

Three weeks later, on a cooler afternoon, I refused an order to shoot at civilians in a vehicle that wouldn't stop at a checkpoint. Five months later, I stood before a military tribunal for failing to obey this order, for failing to be a good soldier.

The 737 taxis out of the gate and onto the tarmac on its way to San Francisco. The fragile skeleton of the aircraft shakes, as if all of its screws are loose. Instructions are given for what to do in case of an emergency. An older man reading *Forbes*, with a trimmed beard and slicked back comb-over, turns and glances at me every once in a while. Does he think I'm going to blow up the plane? The wheels of the aircraft speed up on the runway. The plane shakes with greater vigour. The aircraft climbs the sky. There's no feeling of moving forward. The wings tilt. Around we go, Chicago's city grid visible from the corner of my eye. The trumpets sound from a movement from the *1812 Overture* after a flight attendant's voice drops from the intercom. The universe can no longer be trusted. I'm losing my authority over memory and perception. My mind and body are still primed for lethal danger. Any sound, any element may set me off. The dust of the old place still coats and constricts my throat.

All these people on the plane right now have no idea. They're all proud of me no matter what. They have no idea. And the soldier on the plane, if he knew what I'd not done, would think I'm a coward, which is what I may be. I don't know how the hours pass. Every plane landing is a controlled crash. It's not that different from the re-entry of a soldier back into civilian life. When the plane lands, I have no idea what my life will be like. It will be nothing like the old life. And still, I want to believe I am a good soldier.

FOR DISPLAY PURPOSES ONLY

MARCUS FLEMING

Its top elegantly raised, the baby grand gleamed under an arrangement of little spotlights. The stool was upholstered in studded, oxblood leather. An A4 page was mounted in Perspex and placed on top.

Bill checked in and hurried across the echoing lobby to read the notice. He hoped it would promise a pianist later with a selection of Brahms or Gershwin.

Please DO NOT play the piano.
The piano is for display purposes only.

Bill was offended by the waste of the piano; this proud silent machine, polished and presented like an extinct and stuffed animal.

He went to his room and wandered about, getting his prints on things. He tried all the lights. He took the paper cover from the glass in the bathroom, though he wouldn't be using it. He'd heard tales of overworked cleaners using the same cloth on the lavatory, the shower tray, the drinking glass. He squeezed a towel. He fumbled with the TV remote. He almost mistakenly bought a movie before he found the regular channels. He rolled across the wide, firm bed and stood at the window. Bill liked the room.

Across the grassy valley, grey frost clung on in the long shadows of the bare trees. The far end of the pasture was flooded. Ducks played in the blue water. Cathy would have loved all this. It was a real pity she couldn't make this trip.

Bill was waiting for Rory's call. The lobby bar was a pristine area of minimalist furniture where the cool atmosphere was ruined by the hum of an extractor fan.

—A bottle of beer please. Anything European.

The girl was incredibly thin and had very large lips. She stopped polishing the disassembled parts of a coffee machine. She pointed with her cloth to another A4 mounted page.

THE LOBBY BAR IS CLOSED.
Please join us in the Cellar Bar.

—Okay. I hear ya.

The girl did not reply. Bill, fifty-five this year, supposed he was already partially invisible to her.

He didn't feel like drinking in a basement during the day. Besides, he might not get phone reception and he didn't want Rory leaving long messages.

Bill walked to the lake. His breath wisped ahead of him in white bursts. He stood under a tree. He regretted not having a camera with him. The sunlight was pure on the glade and the huge, gnarled tree was entirely coated with pale, fluffy moss. Wide, drooping green ferns sprouted along the branches. It all had the picturesque quality of one of Cathy's inspirational calendars: *You Are Free.*

Bill remembered then that his phone had a camera and enjoyed himself for a while, taking pictures. Though it was February, he found a few perfect conkers and, on an ancient reflex, pocketed them.

The lake was fringed with ice, eggshell-thin. Bill poked his toe here and there, loving the crackle and crunch. He held up a piece of ice. For all the world it was a perfect sliver of thin glass melting over his hot red fingers. His phone bleated. It was Rory.

—Bill. Running kind of late here. You there already?

—Oh yes.

—You and the missus enjoying it, then?

—Cathy couldn't make it. Her father's not great.

There was no need for details, for Rory to know about a mind in accelerating decline, about a family at war with itself, about another silent piano, this one an upright in a wallpapered parlour overlooking Sandymount Strand and the grey-black Irish Sea.

—So look. Should still make it for dinner. On my way to the airport now.

The lake was serene and perfect. Distant traffic swooshed. A nearby pheasant glucked. Just tell me now, thought Bill. Just say it on the phone and let me go home. On my computer, I'll make a pretty image of that fern-covered tree with an inspirational slogan in white text: *You Are Fired*.

After a short silence, Rory just said righty ho and they both hung up. The cellar bar didn't seem like such a murky prospect anymore.

It turned out to be a beautifully renovated wine cellar. Bill drank a bottle of nice Belgian beer. He had been a young piano man in a hotel bar when he first met Cathy. She admired his playing, laughing as if he was performing magic tricks. That was thirty years ago and Bill was a middleman in the car game now. Rory was in charge of the imports. Bill worked on distribution to dealers. The first hint that Bill was marked as dispensable had come a week ago in a phone conversation with Rory.

—So let's meet up. Cavan. Woods, lakes, a sauna, a few jars. And we'll figure where we go from here. Going forward.

The company was to proceed, pushing their product into an already saturated market. Bill had been first to hear from the forecourts, the dealers. Since the so-called downturn, punters had been sitting tight with whatever wheels they had in the yard.

But the real deathblow, Bill felt, had come with images on the TV news. Brand new cars, untouched and unwanted in deep-perspective parade formations, crowding shipyards all over the world. Thousands of neat rows of cars, each one as pristine and wasted as that lovely piano upstairs.

In the sauna, a good-looking young Northern couple chatted in outdoor tones. Bill left them to it. He tried the laconium but it was hardly as warm as Cathy's little greenhouse in Dublin. Alone in his trunks on a tiled bench in the lukewarm dark, Bill felt bored and silly.

The steam room was more the job. The wet heat flushed through his nose with a menthol rush and seared his throat. The centre of the steam room was clumsily occupied by a stand displaying a giant illuminated photo of pine cones.

Bill hosed himself a little with cold water and sat back, listening to his own steady breath and the sigh of the steam. He contemplated his drooping oval gut, his whitening chest hair, his breasts, sagging like empty goat's udders, his crimson knees. He had to watch the blood pressure but he wasn't in terrible shape. He ate a lot of fruit. Cathy encouraged him to try new things. Bill was grateful for his body. It had not betrayed him at all, really. One of his shoulders wasn't worth a goddamn. But so what? He was no longer into heavy-lifting or basketball.

He lolled his head in a circle, cracking his neck. He would pitch his idea to Rory over dinner that night. The big idea first came to him while watching the unwanted cars on the news.

He rose into a defensive boxing pose, swaying a little in the steam. His idea could save his job. His feet pattered on the puddled tiles. He threw a left through the clouds. He turned, following his imaginary opponent. He snorted and threw a short right upper cut.

Bill's idea could get him promoted. He just needed to pitch it well that night. He needed to pitch it as perfectly as this knockout punch charging forward in the scalding steam. The door was open and the good-looking Northern couple stared as Bill's fist collided with the pine cones photo.

In the thick robe and white slippers, Bill relaxed onto the bed. He slept.

The phone rang and the bedside table was in the wrong place. He grasped only empty space. He remembered where he was, the hotel, and found the phone. Cathy was put through.

—I decided to call you on the landline. Cheaper. On our deal. You know the way.

—Very economical.

—These days.

—These days. How's your dad?

Cathy groaned.

—He came. The tuner.

—Good. How'd it go?

—Not great. Pretty awful really.

Bill felt a rush of guilt. The piano tuner had been his idea. Cathy's parents had both played. But after her mother passed on, the old upright was only attacked by bored and giddy grandchildren during enforced visits. It was out of tune beyond all recognition, an aural nightmare that Bill could not disassociate from his father-in-law's encroaching dementia. So Bill suggested the piano tuner. A little piano music in the parlour might give the old boy some pleasure, perhaps even return a few happy memories.

—I introduced the piano tuner to Daddy and that was fine, but then Daddy forgot about him and later, he was going by the room and heard the piano. He looks in and there's this stranger. When I got there, Daddy was swinging the poker at him. The tuner's mostly blind so he was a bit shook too.

—Did he hit him?

—No, thank God.

—Sorry, Cath. I thought it would work out.

Bill wished he was there with Cathy, instead of in a bland, plush hotel room with fat pillows, waiting for Rory to fire him.

—I'm not finished. When Daddy got up again later on, he'd forgotten all about the tuner and I played him a bit of 'Für Elise'. He started crying.

—Oh, man.

—No. He really liked it. He was happy. Humming along a bit.

Cathy lilted a bar of the tune. From nowhere, a sob expanded in Bill's throat. He coughed. He told her about the piano in the hotel with the stupid sign. She laughed.

—Did you tell Rory your big idea?

—He's not here yet. Held up.

—Right, well, the company can't be that badly off anyway. Spa breaks in places with laconiums. Did you find out what that was?

—It's a kind of Roman sauna. Didn't rate it really. Maybe it wasn't switched on. Cath, did you inquire about the nurse?

—Yes. It hasn't gotten any cheaper.

Bill said nothing while he burrowed a knuckle into a pillow. Cathy spoke low.

—Maybe if you got a promotion after your idea.

Bill should never have told Cathy about his idea. She didn't know it was just a final flourish, a last claw-swipe for survival.

—Your father's money. Did you say about that to Alice?

Alice was Cathy's sister, divorced and spiteful.

—She just keeps saying we're managing fine with Daddy ourselves. Why throw his money away?

—She means her inheritance.

Cathy kept her silence, then brightened.

—Don't drink too much tonight now, you.

—Don't worry. We'll just have dinner and a few scoops.

—The piano tuner was a great idea, Bill.

—I'm an ideas man.

Bill drank alone and ate a sandwich that tasted of nothing but the salt and pepper he added. He went to the toilets and experienced a mild feeling of physical levitation. When he got back, he checked the Belgian beer label. Nine per cent.

—I might as well be drinking pints of wine.

The friendly barman's shift ended. He was replaced by the speechless lean girl with the big lips. Bill ordered a water. His phone rang and he resisted pouncing too quickly. It was Rory, no doubt to say he was on the road.

—Not looking good, Bill.

—How so?

—Hassle at the airport. A mess up over being understaffed or something. The flight's delayed. Cancelled. I don't know in Christ what.

Bill said nothing.

—So I don't know what time I'm gonna get there. If I'm gonna get there. At best it'll be late tonight. Too late to meet up. What do you think of a breakfast meeting?

—Whatever works for you, Rory. I'm here.

Bill realised Rory was probably not even at Manchester airport. He was talking so much, it just had to be a lie.

—Cos I don't know. Way it's looking now. Don't know if I'm gonna get up in the air tonight. Wee hours maybe.

He wanted Bill to say 'Leave it. I understand.' It was now or never, Bill realised.

—Rory. I've got this idea.

Rory was hissing at somebody about how he wanted his coffee prepared.

—I've got this idea. It could make a big difference. The company.

—I'm all ears.

He was not. But Bill unfolded his notes and ploughed on.

—The cars in Cork say. They're pretty typical of what's happening everywhere right? These cars just sitting there, costing rental space. Two and a half thousand of them. Last I counted.

Rory grunted.

Bill became conscious of his booze-thickened tongue, the beginning of a slur. He sipped water and fought on, a hand over his eyes.

—Those cars. My idea starts with writing them off. Not the cars but the profit on them. I'm not a marketing man, Rory, but I know this is a marketing man's world. So this is mostly a marketing idea.

—I'm kind of following. Look, Bill, can we pick this up...

—This is about how the car industry is perceived by people in the western world right now. More and more, cars are just seen as part of the problem. Oil guzzling old machines, adding to global warming. All that. But if we take this current crisis and turn it into an opportunity. We can be the car company with the best public image when people start buying cars again.

Rory's coffee had arrived and he slurped discreetly.

—I'm listening.

—We send the cars to poor countries in Africa. Or some other Godforsaken hole. Maybe South America.

—That's what you mean by write off?

—Yes. We become the car company that's dealing with the coalface problem in the developing world. Transport.

—Is that the coalface problem in the developing world?

—I don't know. But I saw on the news, two hundred people and their luggage swinging off a truck in a desert. Looked like a transport problem to me.

—What then?

—We give away a few thousand cars that we can't sell anyway. We sell the next wave of cars at cost. We prioritise hybrid engines. We brand the whole thing the way they brand fairtrade coffee. Big marketing push to show we're doing it. Part of the future. Not the past.

—Jesus, Bill.

—We sell cars at cost price in these countries. We build a brand loyalty with the world's fastest growing populations.

—Right. I get you.

—The home market. The Western World. We improve their perception of us, a massive marketing campaign. Advertising. Kids getting to hospital. Skinny black lads getting to work. I don't know. We tie sales in. For every five cars we sell in Ireland, we send a car to the developing world.

There was a ticking noise at Rory's end and Bill realised he was typing.

—Bill. It's a good idea. I think it's a fucking zinger.

Rory was only forty. He said things like 'zinger'. Bill knew the sound of a sale made. He relaxed a little.

—There's a Nigerian guy, name is Pius, below in Cork. He ships bangers back home. Wrecked engines, everything. He knows people who can help with the other end. They'll work with us, Rory. I think the idea should be perceived to have started small like that. More of a people thing than a corporate thing.

—It's a really good idea, Bill.

He didn't need to say 'but'. Bill did it for him.

—But.

—They've already decided. They had to make fast, ruthless decisions. Job specs like yours just didn't survive the scrutiny. I don't think they saw ideas like this coming from someone like you.

Bill flapped a hand at the skinny girl with the big lips. He pointed at the nine per cent empty, nodded. She fetched one.

—I'm sorry, Bill.

—I hear ya, Rory.

Bill drank the nine per cent beer from the bottle and it tasted like water.

*

Bill switched to whiskey and ice when his belt buckle started grooving into his belly. The lean girl with the big lips was good at her job and soon only a finger twitch was needed to have his glass refilled. He signed each bill to the room until his signature was worse than a doctor's.

At the next table, the Northern couple barked away and Bill took to raising his drinks to them. A trip to the toilets was like a fever dream. He almost fell asleep with his face on the hand dryer.

Bill drank and his thoughts curdled, turning from Rory, sure to take credit for the big idea, to Alice, the sister-in-law witch, too greedy to have her own father cared for properly and then to Philip, Bill's son, ungrateful and ashamed of his parents, forever absent.

Bill wanted to phone Cathy but knew he was so drunk it would scare the poor woman. Instead, he sat, silently drinking, his mind bathed for just a while in a stupid, gurgling happy affection.

Bill nodded thank you to the skinny bar girl and was seized by a puzzle. The girl's origin. Poland? Estonia? It seemed suddenly urgent. Bill tried to ask.

—I wanted. I wanted. I wanted to know what you. Where you. If. How long.

It was no use. Her eyebrows squirmed with pity but she said nothing. Bill tipped her a fiver and went to the stairs.

Outside, a fresh drizzle embraced him and he raised his arms.

Rory would use Bill's idea. But if it went into action, it could do good.

Alice was tortured by her own obvious failings and crippled by paranoia. She would help with the nursing fees. Bill would just have to sell the idea to her.

Philip was young, just beginning as a solicitor in a world that must seem impossibly crowded with problems. Bill turned in the drizzle and remembered his son's beardless little face, frowning in capable labour over a book of sums.

—Love.

Bill was cold now, his shirt drenched. Enough. He went back to the hotel and straight to the piano. It was as smooth and serene and dark and beautiful as the lake.

Bill sat. He put the Perspex sign on the floor behind the piano. He called to the new girl on reception.

—*Cavatina* by John Williams. Better known as *The Deerhunter*. My own arrangement.

Bill flicked off a salute. He began to play. He didn't tinkle about either. He went straight in hard and hit those first chords. You don't test drive a new car in a car park.

—It's in tune. By God it is.

Bill realised he was a half-step high and stopped.

—Do over.

—Sir. The piano is not supposed to be played.

But the piano keys were narrow. No. Bill's fingers were a little thick and stiff, especially the middle one on the left that got hurt in today's steam room brawl.

—This is really not working. Sorry.

—Sir. It's very late. Please.

—Yes. I'm trying, sorry. I think I was too slow as well. Onetwothreefour. And there we are.

Bill went at it again.

—Sir.

This time, he nailed it. Just nailed it. It was a wonderful piano with a massive sound and the marble-clad lobby loved it. Bill let his hands follow where they were sent. He found the music worked better when he roared along with it. He'd never been much of a singer, but then maybe the songs had never been this true.

The receptionist fetched the shy and gigantic night porter.

Bill pounded the keys, his fingers aflame in the bones. Bill roared some more. It was pretty fucking good.

—That's enough, sir.

—Just let me finish my song.

—Sir. That's enough. You have to stop. People are trying to sleep.

—I hear ya. Everybody's asleep. That's the problem.

The night porter wore glistening, hard-toed brogues.

—Sir. It's after midnight.

—It's getting late, alright.

—I'm going to remove you from the piano, sir.

—You're gonna try.

Bill thumped those keys. The only thing for it, the only way to make the wonder of it make sense, was to roar some more.

The porter lifted Bill under the arms.

—Sir. It's over.

He pulled Bill backwards from the piano. The song was not finished. With a last outstretched hand, Bill flicked at the keys, bellowing.

—Why can't you leave him at it for one minute? He's had a bad day.

It was the lean girl with the big lips. She had a strong Dublin accent. She was near the stairs, gripping a rail.

The good-looking Northern couple stood at the desk with the receptionist.

Rory had arrived. He posed just inside the main door, his suit bag strapped across his chest, laptop case on the floor, car keys glinting in his hand. Hot and wet, Bill struggled in the porter's arm lock and everybody stared.

THE GIRLS AND THE DOGS
KEVIN BARRY

I was living in a caravan a few miles outside Gort. It was set up on breeze blocks in the yard of an old farmhouse. There were big nervous dogs outside, chained. Their breathing caught hard with the cold of the winter and the way the wind shuddered along their flanks was wretched to behold. I lay there in the night, as the dogs howled misery at the darkness, and I doted over a picture of my daughter, May-Anne, as she had been back in the summertime. I hadn't seen her in eight months and I missed her so badly. I was keeping myself well hidden. Things had gone wrong in Cork and then they went wronger again. I had been involved with bringing some of the brown crack in that was said to be causing people to have strokes and was said to have caused the end altogether of a prostitute lad on Douglas Street. Everybody was looking for me. There was no option for a finish only to hop on a bus and then it was all black skies and bogger towns and Gort, finally, and Evan the Head waited for me there, in the ever-falling rain, and he had his bent smile on.

'Here's another one I got to weasel you out of,' he said. 'And me without the arse o' me fuckin' kecks, 'ay?'

He jerked a thumb at a scabby Fiesta that wore no plates and we climbed into it and took off through the rain, January, and we drove past wet fields and stone walls and he asked me no questions at all. He said it was often the way that a fella needed a place and he would be glad to help me out. He said that I was his friend after all and he softened the word in his mouth—friend—in a way that I found troubling. It was the softness that named the price of the word. He said things could as easily be the other way around and maybe someday I would be there to help him out. He said if he didn't see me at the swings, he would meet me on the roundabouts. We turned down a crooked boreen that ran between fields left to reeds and there were no people anywhere to be seen. We came to the farmhouse and the smile on the Head's face twisted even more so.

'I never promised you a rose garden,' he said.

You would have hardly thought it held anyone at all but for the yellow screams of the children escaping the torn curtains and the filthy windows. Evan said he had rent allowance got for the house on account of his children. He had bred six off Suze and a couple off her sister, Elsie. These were open-minded people I was dealing with. At least with regard to that end of things. We went inside and the kids appeared everywhere, they were shaven-headed against the threat of nits, and they were pelting about like maniacs, grinding their teeth and hammering at the walls, and the women appeared—girlish, Elsie and Suze, as thin as girls—and they smirked at me in a particular way over the smoke of their roll-ups: it is through no fault of my own that I am considered a very handsome man.

'Coffee and buns, no?' said Evan the Head, and the girls laughed.

The house was in desperate shape. There were giant mushroom-shaped damp patches coming through the old wallpaper and a huge fireplace in the main room was burning a fire made of smashed up chairs and bits of four-be-two. The Head wasn't lying when he said I'd be as well off outside in the caravan. He brought me to it and I was relieved to get out to the yard, mainly because of the kids, who had a real viciousness to them.

Now of course the caravan was no mansion either. The door's lock was busted and the door was tied shut with a piece of chain left over from the dogs and fixed with a padlock. The dogs were big and of hard breeds but they were nervous, fearful, and they backed away into the corners of the yard as we passed by. Evan unlooped the chain and opened the door and with a flourish bid me enter.

'Can you smell the sex off it?' he said, climbing in behind.

'Go 'way?'

'Bought it off a brasser used to work the horse fairs,' he said. 'If the walls could talk in this old wagon, 'ay?'

It had a knackery look to it, sure enough. It was an old sixteen-footer aluminium job with a flowery carpet rotten away to fuck and flouncy pillows with the flounce gone out of them and it reeked of the fields and winter. There was a wee gas fire with imitation logs. Evan got down and sparked the fire with his lighter.

'Get you good an' cosy,' he said. 'You any money, boy-child?'

'I've about three euro odd, Ev.'

'Captain of industry,' he said.

The gas fire got going and the fumes rose from it so hard they watered my eyes. I asked was it safe and he said it'd be fine, it'd be balmy, it'd be like I was on my holidays, and if I got bored, I could always pop inside the house and see if young Elsie fancied a lodger.

'For her stomach,' he said.

I am not lying when I tell you there was a time Evan the Head was thought to be a bit of a charmer. He was from Swansea originally and sometimes in his cups he would talk about it like it was a kind of paradise and his accent would come through stronger. I had known him five years and I would have to say he was a mysterious character. I had met him first in a pub on Barrack Street in Cork called The Three Ones. It wasn't a pub that had the best of names for itself. It was a rough crowd that drank there and there was an amount of dealing that went on and an amount of feuds on account of the dealing. There had been shootings the odd time. I was nervous there always but Evan was calm and smiling at the barside and one night I went back to the flat he had in Togher and I bought three sheets of acid off him at a good price—White Lightnings, ferocious visuals—and he showed me passports for himself that were held under three different names. I was young enough to be impressed by that though I have seen quarer sights since, believe me. Evan used to talk about orgies all the time. He would go on and on about organising a good proper orgy—'ay?—and he told me once about an orgy in a graveyard in Swansea that himself and an old girlfriend had set up and that's when he started taking down Aleister Crowley books about the occult and telling me he suspected I might be a white witch.

Magick, said Evan, should be always written with the extra 'k'.

I emptied out my bag in the caravan—it held just a few pairs of boxer shorts and T-shirts and trackie pants. I had little enough by way of possessions since Fiona Condon had turfed me out, the lighting bitch. I had not arranged to collect my stuff. I would not give her the satisfaction, her and her barring order, and I was dressing myself out of Penneys. She hadn't let me near my daughter, I hadn't seen May-Anne since the day in June I had taken her out to the beach at Garrettstown. Evan watched me as I unpacked my few bits and I felt by his quietness that he was sorrowful for me. At least I hoped that was what the quietness was.

'Have you any food, Ev?' I said.

'You not eaten?'

I told him I'd made it from Cork on the strength of a banana and a Snickers bar.

'Poor starving little wraith,' he said.

He said I could come in later. He said there would be a pot of curried veg on the go. And that was the way our routine began, so simply. I would come in, the evenings, and I would be fed, and I would watch TV for a while and help with burning the four-be-twos before going and dry-humping Elsie on a mattress in a back room that smelled of kid piss and dried blood.

Elsie the third night told me that she loved me.

Now Elsie to this day I do not believe had original badness in her. It was just that she could be easily led and her sister had badness in her sure enough and as for Evan, well.

I said, the third night:

'But Elsie you're fleadhin' Ev and all, yeah?'

'What's fleadhin'?' she said.

'Fuckin'',' I said. 'It's a Cork word for fuckin'.'

'Business o' yours how?' she said.

Elsie and Suze were from Leeds—Leeds-Irish—but they had people in south Galway. Their father was put away for knocking their mother unconcious with the welt of a slap-hammer and they turned up on the doorstep of the Galway cousins and they were turned away again lively. Their eyes were too dark and their mouths were too beautiful. They were the kind of girls—women—who look kind of dramatic and unsafe. They were at a loose end arsing around Galway then, fucking Australians out of youth hostels and robbing them, and they met Evan the Head in the Harbour Bar, was the story, when there still was a Harbour Bar, before the Galway docks was all cunts in pink shirts drinking wine. Evan was loaded at that time having brought in a trawler full of grade-two resin from Morocco—he came into Doolin with it, bold as brass, stoned as a coot in the yellow of his oilskins—and that was ten years back and if one of the sisters wasn't up the spout off him since, the other was.

'Evan an' me is over,' said Elsie, 'but I'm not sayin' he isn't a wonderful father.'

At that moment there was the loud cracking sound of wood snapping—*shhlaaack!*—which meant that Evan the Head had lain a length of four-be-two along the bottom steps of the stairs and taken a lep at it from the banister. He was a limber man and he enjoyed breaking up the firewood in this way.

See him perched up on the banister, with the weird grin on, and he eyeing just the spot where he wanted to crack the wood—then the wee lep.

In Cork I had seen Suze sure enough, smothered by children and dope smoke on the couch of the Togher flat, but I had never seen Elsie though I had heard her, once, in a far room, crying.

'Does Suze love him still do you think?'

'No,' said Elsie, 'but he has the spell on her, don't he? I can beat the spell.'

So it was—so simple—that we became a kind of family that January in the old farmhouse outside Gort. But of course I could not say I was ever entirely comfortable with the situation. I kept going out to the caravan at night, to be alone for those cold hours, for my own space and to think of May-Anne, to look at her photograph, and to listen to the dogs, the strange comfort of them. Elsie thought this was snobbish of me. She wanted me to stay with her on the mattress. And Evan the Head said he agreed with her, and Suze agreed, and that was the start of the trouble.

But I'm getting ahead of myself. I want to tell you about Elsie and what she looked like when she came. She wouldn't allow me to put it inside because there'd been complications with the last child she'd had bred off her for Evan and she didn't want another kid happening. I said fine to that. I have never been comfortable with being a father. I love May-Anne—my dotey pet, I always call her—but it makes me frightened just to think of her walking around in the world with the people that are out there. See some of the fuckers you'd have muttering at the walls down around the bus station in Parnell Place, Cork. You'd want a daughter breathing the same air as those animals?

'Get in there my son!' Ev cried from the hallway into the back room where Elsie and I lay on the mattress. 'Get in!'

When she came Elsie had a tic beneath her left eye—at the top of her cheek there was a fluttering as if a tiny bird was caught beneath her skin. The dry-humping made me feel like a teenager again but not in a good way. We lay there—a particular night—with Elsie's tic going, with me all handsome and useless, and Evan leapt on the four-be-twos off the banister, and the eight mad kids bounced off the ceilings and bit each other and screamed, and the wind howled outside, and the wretched dogs cried a great howling in answer to the wind, and then Suze was at the door, and she said:

'Why don't we make this interestin'?'

Yes it started like that—the trouble—it started as a soft kind of coaxing. Sly comments from Suze and sly comments from Evan the Head. And I got worried when the winter stretched on, the weeks threw down their great length, the weeks were made of sleet and wind, and it became February—a hard month—and the sly comments came even from Elsie then. She was easily led and bored enough for badness. I started to feel a bit trapped in this place and I thought about moving on but I had nowhere to go and no money to get there. Given the way things had turned out in Cork, I would be shot or arrested if I went back, no question. I missed May-Anne—it was hell—but I thought the best I could do for her was to keep myself safe until the troubled times had passed over.

Then, late one night, Evan the Head came into the yard—I heard him hiss at the dogs. Without so much as a knock he was in the door of the caravan. He sat on the foot of my fold-out bed. He lit a candle and I saw him by its soft light. He had his twisted smile on. First words he said to me:

'Suze is the better comer.'

'Go 'way?'

'Know what a geyser is?'

'I do, yeah.'

'That's Suze if she's in the form. You see she's got one eye a dark brown and one a dark, really dark green?'

'Yeah, kinda …'

'Yeah kinda noticed that, 'ay? Did you, boy?'

'Yeah.'

'Yeah, well that's a good sign,' he said, 'for a comer.'

I did not reply because I did not like the way he was smoking his roll-up. The hard little sucks on it and his eyes so deep-set.

'She's inside,' he said.

I said nothing.

'I said she's waitin' on you, boy. Are you goin' to keep her waitin'?'

'Ah please, Ev.'

'You don't want to get that lady riled. Suze? Not a good plan, boy-child. I said you don't get that fucking lady riled!'

'Evan, look, I've the thing with her sister, haven't I?'

He stood then—he loomed in the candlelight—and the words that came were half-hissed, half-whispered:

'You'll get in that fucking house and you'll fuck my wife and you'll fuck her sister or you'll get the fucking life taken out of you, d'ya hear me, boy?'

'Evan get out of the caravan, please!'

He leapt up on the bed then and he danced about and he laughed so hard. And he kind of poked at my head with his feet, kind of playful, as if he was going to stamp me, but then he let it go, he stood down, and he left without another word. Then I heard him turn the padlock on the chain outside.

They kept me locked in the caravan for days and nights I quickly lost the count of. The windows were rusted shut and could not be squeezed back and I was so weak because they brought me no food and no water. I was in a bad state very quickly. The dogs outside I believe sensed that I was weakening, that I was dying, and they called to me. We were held on the same length of chain. In the daytime the girls came and whispered through the door to me—awful, filthy stuff that I would not repeat, for hours they whispered—and I knew that Elsie hadn't the better of the spell anymore. Evan came by night and he crawled over the roof of the caravan and he made little tapping noises. I roared and cried myself hoarse but there was no one to hear me out there and after a few days I was slipping in and out of a desperate weird sleep—full of sour, scary dreams, like bad whiskey dreams—and I felt the cold of the fields come into my bones and once in the afternoon dusk I woke from a fever to find Evan the Head outside a window of the caravan and in each of his arms he held a child to look in at me, and I knew it was the first time ever that I had seen those children calm. I have never had religion or spiritual feelings but lying there in the caravan in the farmyard outside Gort I knew for sure there was no God but there was surely a devil.

But if I gritted my teeth against the fear and kept my eyes clamped tightly shut, the sweats would seem to ease off for a while and I would see clearly the day on the beach with May-Anne, at Garretstown, in the early summer. It was a windy, blustery day, but the sea and the sand made us high, we were soaring, and we ran about like mad things on the beach. Afterwards, before the bus back to town, I bought her a 99 at a seaside shop. The shop had all sorts of beach tat for sale and she asked me about the porkpie hats that said 'kiss-me-quick'.

'What's kiss-me-quick?'

'It's just a seaside thing,' I said. 'An old saying. From England I think.'

'Kiss-me-quick kiss-me-quick kiss-me-quick,' she said it in a duck's voice from a cartoon and I pecked her on the cheek, really quickly, peck peck peck, and I nuzzled the nape of her neck, she squealed.

I don't know how many days I had been locked in the caravan when I crawled the length of it one morning and under the sink found two tins of Campbell's Cream of Tomato soup from years ago, probably, from the days of the brasser I would say. I opened them and drank them cold and it was a horrible taste, it made me retch, but I kept the soup down and if I did not come to life exactly it felt as if my thoughts came for a short while in a clearer, more realistic way.

There was a closet in the caravan with a chemical toilet I had never used because of the smell—it was better to piss in the yard— but now I realised when I lifted up the toilet that plenty had used it before me, and the piss and Domestos that had seeped and spilled from it over the years had left the floorboards beneath badly rotten. They were rotten to the extent that some had been replaced with a piece of ply.

I waited until the night. Elsie and Suze had come just once in the afternoon to whisper their filth at me, and Evan had on the roof for a while made his tap-tappings and I realised then he was working from some kind of Aleister Crowley book—magick—and when he went away I waited, waited, until all in the farmhouse was darkness and quiet, and there was just the feeling of the dogs outside.

I crawled into the toilet room and pushed back the chemical loo and the ply beneath came loose so easily it was unreal, it was like wet cardboard in my hands. The hole I quickly made was no more than two, two and a half foot wide, but that was enough to squeeze through, and I was crawling along the wet ground of the yard then beneath the caravan. All of the dogs huddled close to the ground and peered at me, oh and their eyes—so yellow—were livid, but they made not a sound, they were as quiet as the air was cold.

I wriggled out from beneath the caravan and sat with my back to it to ease the beating of my heart. No lights came on in the farmhouse and the dogs so quietly watched me as I found the strength to walk to the Fiesta and I climbed into it. I lifted off the panel for the wires to come loose and I knew well enough which of the wires to rub together.

I was no more than halfways down the crooked boreen when the lights came on in the farmhouse and there were roars and screams and the sound of doors and footsteps and with my eyes pinned I steered along till the boreen gave onto road and I missed the verge and the tyre ripped on rocks but I kept going hard into the night. The way the ripped rubber of the tyre slapped along the back road had a rhythm to it—three beats, again and again and again—and I heard it as kiss-me-quick, kiss-me-quick, and I drove it until the screaming of the voices—oh May-Anne—and the footsteps behind had faded—my sweetheart, my dotey—to nothing, just nothing at all, and I was at a high vantage suddenly and beneath me, on a plain, were the lights of Gort.

THE KILLER AND HIS LITTLE FRIEND

ZAKHAR PRILEPIN

Translated from the Russian by Philip Ó Ceallaigh

We were *Spetsnaz* reservists, deployed as back-up on the capital's highway. There were three of us: Sereoga, who went by the nickname 'Ape,' his pal Gnome, and me.

Ape had recently bought himself sixteen kilos of cartridges from a regular soldier and each time he went on duty he'd grab a fistful like they were sunflower seeds. He'd loaded his service weapon and was looking about for something to shoot at.

Around three in the morning, when there weren't many cars, Ape saw a stray dog traversing the road. Bad luck for the dog. He whistled at it. The dog seemed suspicious, then it tried to sidle up to people who smelled of badness and steel and, of course, took a fatal bullet in its side.

The dog didn't die straight away, though. It spent a good while whining. Loud enough to wake half the forest.

The checkpoint building was next to a forest.

I spat my cigarette, took a gulp of air and went off to drink some tea.

'I suppose it'll get its brains blown out now,' I thought, tensing in anticipation, even though I'd had shots fired around me, I don't know, maybe ten thousand times.

It rattled me this time too, but at least it put a stop to the dog.

I wasn't angry with Ape, and wasn't particularly sorry for the dog. So, he'd killed it. The guy liked shooting, and that's all there was to it.

'I wouldn't mind a revolution,' Ape told me once.

'Really?' I exclaimed, happy; I wanted a revolution too.

'Yeah. I'd get my fill of shooting,' he replied. It took me a second to realise just what it was he wanted to kill.

Even then I wasn't too bothered. Basically, I was fond of Ape. Undercover maniacs passing for humans, that's what's revolting. But Ape was straight up about his passions and I didn't see anything nasty in his particular way of doing things, and in addition he was clearly a good soldier. Sometimes I think that's how soldiers should be, like Ape—the rest sooner or later turn out to be good for nothing.

On top of that, he had a great sense of humour and was very easy-going. In fact, that's the only thing about men that I find appealing: their capacity to be couragous and cheerful. Their other qualities impress me less.

Ape's nickname never bothered him. Particularly after I explained that apes were related both to humans and monkeys. And the Australian sloth.

But his take was completely different: he maintained that all the other fighters in the unit descended from him.

'I'm your great-grandfather, you tailless monkeys,' Ape would say, with infectious laughter.

Gnome, meanwhile, joked he was Ape's father, though he was only a third of his height.

Ape weighed a hundred and twenty kilos and could knock anyone in the unit flat. Personally, I wouldn't have tried taking him on. In wrestling sessions he wasn't called to the mat, having on one occasion broken someone's ribs and on another injured somebody's head, both times in the first moments of the engagement.

Until Gnome joined the unit, Ape didn't spend time talking with anyone in particular: he pumped iron, laughed and was equally friendly with everyone.

But he made friends with Gnome.

Gnome was the shortest member of the unit and I've never understood how he got selected: we had a few guys who weren't so tall, but they were all built like monsters.

But Gnome really was a gnome, his hands were slender and his ribcage was like a birdcage.

At first I didn't spare him a second glance, and I don't even remember when he appeared among us, which I'm sure suited him fine. Maybe he was keeping a low profile. But later, over a smoke, we got talking and I learned that his wife had recently left him. She'd been raised in an orphanage and never managed to settle down and adapt to marriage and domesticity. So he ended up on his own with their six-year-old daughter and that was how it was for a time; father and daughter, living together. Fortunately, Gnome's mother lived in a house nearby and would drop by and feed the little one while her son, the abandoned husband, was off working.

Telling me this, Gnome didn't make a big deal of his fate or get melancholy, he just drew hard on his cigarette as though he wanted to turn it to ash in one go. He didn't succeed in one, but after five he was down to the filter.

A feeling of sympathy for him was awoken in me. And after that I would observe the pair of them, Ape and Gnome. They ate together, smoked together and near enough took trips to the toilet together. Soon they were even driving around, picking up low women, sometimes one between the two of them, sometimes stuffing more of them in the vehicle than you could count, all of them screaming and laughing their heads off; and it made no difference that Ape himself had an attractive young wife.

Ape, despite the nickname, had a big white hairless face. His features were rather spread out, so when he smiled it seemed as if everything was reverting to normal—the nose reasserted itself, the eyes became alert, the Adam's apple protruded, and his mouth became full of chunky big yellow teeth.

Gnome didn't have a beard either, but he sported a narrow

moustache, officer style. Everything about his face was small, which made him look like a funny moustachioed doll. And when Gnome smiled, it was impossible to distinguish his features. They suddenly mixed together and blended, his eyes disappeared somewhere, and he gnashed his mouthful of little teeth.

Unlike Ape, Gnome didn't appear bloodthirsty; even though he had no trouble watching. He personally didn't plan killing anybody, but he observed his big pal's passion with interest, as though sizing something up, looking at it from different angles.

From the guard-post, I could heard their excited voices in the street. I went outside.

'Did you kill the dog?' I asked.

'A bitch,' replied Ape, with satisfaction.

He raised his gun, as though it was itching, flicked the safety catch, placed it against one of the wooden posts supporting the porch—it was as wide as a good-sized birch—and fired again.

'Look at that,' he said, checking the pillar. 'It didn't go through. Gnome, why don't you lean on the other side, and I'll give it another go?'

'Go press your own palm against it!' said Gnome, grinning.

Ape applied his palm to the pillar and placed the barrel of the gun on the side opposite his enormous paw and quickly fired again. I was seized by some superstitious fear and it all happened before I could utter a word. I didn't see if his hand jumped or not when he fired, because I blinked. As I opened my eyes, Ape was slowly lifting his supporting hand. He looked at it, bringing it close up to his eyes. It was white and clean.

In the morning, at the base, we were met by Ape's wife. Her face was tender, damp and sleepy, like a flower after rain. She looked like she'd been crying and hadn't slept.

'Where were you?' she asked her husband—a stupid question—stepping up to him. They looked good together, both long-legged and strong. They could have been workhorses.

'Fishing, obviously,' he said, irritated, slapping the butt of his pistol.

She broke into fresh tears and, observing Gnome, almost shouted:

'And he's still around. It's all because of him!'

Gnome shrank back from her, his face tensing and becoming as small as Ape's fist.

'Are you crazy?' said Ape indifferently. 'What's your problem? That I have work to do?'

'And you want to go to Chechnya, you bastard,' said the wife, ignoring his question.

Ape shrugged and went to hand in his weapon.

'Can't you say something to him?' she said to me.

'What can I say?'

I reckoned she was mad with jealousy, and with good reason, in believing he was chasing girls instead of going out to work; but her last words concerned Chechnya. What does Chechnya have to do with it? I wondered, answering one question and coming up with another.

The wife waved her hand in disgust, as though dismissing me and my words, and walked away. Oblivious to the cars, she slowly crossed the road and stopped in front of the park, with her back to the base. She stood there, her body swaying slightly.

'She's waiting for him,' I thought to myself, pleased, 'but she wants him to make the first move. Fine woman.'

Handing in his weapon, Ape smoked with Gnome, glancing at his wife's back out the corner of his eye. They laughed, remembering the dog that had been shot, and ground out their cigarette butts under the toes of their boots. They each lit up another cigarette and parted.

Ape went up to his wife and stroked her back.

She said something in reply, perhaps something unpleasant and, without turning around, set off down the road. Ape followed, in no great hurry.

They'll make up after fifty metres, I concluded. I was watching through the window.

Within a minute, Ape had caught up with her and put his hand on her shoulder. She didn't brush it away. I could even sense the swaying of her hips becoming more pronounced—just enough for her hips to brush Ape's.

They'll sort things out as soon as they get home, I thought, sentimentally, provoked by the sight of them. They had a timeless air, like wild creatures.

I knew somehow that Ape had more than the usual degree of male passion. He was as hungry for women as he was thirsty for blood. If it wasn't the one it was the other. That's how it goes.

And Ape was the first to kill someone.

He'd been unhappy all the first week: the streets weren't running with blood. He gazed hungrily at the Chechen landscape, the dramatic scenes of ruin and grim deserted houses, hoping in every moment for gunfire. But nobody fired at him, and he was nervous and irritable with everyone in the unit. Except Gnome, of course. When Ape was talking with him his face became warm and his expression luminous.

The others were practically praying nothing would befall the unit, and this infuriated Ape.

'You've gone to war and don't want to see action?'

'You want to go home in a box?' they asked him.

'What the fuck does it matter how I go home?' he replied.

There was continual firing in the streets around us. Every day Spetsnaz troops in units nearby got killed. Sometimes a whole group of drunk enlisted men would be wiped out in some stupid, absurd firefight. We alone seemed to float through Grozny as though charmed: our unit was mostly involved in escort duties, and sometimes in raids.

Ape often requested we make a detour through a neighbouring street, through the obstinate rattling and spitting of gunfire, as we went around town in an armoured car on missions that never entirely made sense—like going from one godforsaken outpost to another to communicate an order, or deliver a package or a crate of cognac from some major to, let's say, a regiment.

'Fuck it, why there?' I replied from the front seat, to his suggestion that we make a diversion.

'Maybe Russians are getting cut to pieces,' said Ape, grimacing.

'Nobody's being cut to pieces,' I replied. I paused, then added, 'If we're called there, then we'll go.'

Of course, they didn't call us.

But, on the third day of the third week, at the break of dawn on the edge of the city, we finally succeeded in finding three frightened and unarmed men hiding in the attic of a five-storey building. We'd received reports from nearby units of occasional fire coming from the attic.

'Why are you sleeping here?' asked the commanding officer.

'House bombed. Nowhere to sleep,' one of them answered.

The officer ripped the jumper off one of them and the bruise on his shoulder from the recoil of the rifle settled the matter.

But we found no arms in the attic.

'Any ID?' I asked them.

'Burnt in the bombardment!' the Chechens insisted.

'Headquarters can sort that out,' said the commanding officer. 'Split them up so they can't talk,' he ordered. 'So they can't concoct a story.'

Our boys in camouflage spread out and got to work on the building's other stairways. Even from the street you could hear the sound of the occasional door being knocked from its hinges—if no one answered, they kicked them in. The prisoners were separated, and Ape and Gnome got one of them.

I followed the three of them to the double row of sheds beside the building to keep guard, just in case. You never knew when some son of a bitch might surprise you by leaping out from the sheds.

Just as I turned around, lighting up, it suddenly hit me: I remembered the flash in Ape's eyes when he seized the prisoner by the collar and said, 'Let's go,' taking the suspect away from the building that was being raided and towards a patch of waste ground that had lately become a rubbish tip.

I took several steps, and when I looked behind the sheds I saw Ape standing with his back to me and Gnome giving me a dirty look.

'Run,' said Ape, in a low clear voice, 'or else they'll kill you.' 'I'll say you escaped. Run.'

'Stop!' I shouted, choking with horror.

The Chechen took off at my shout, darting through the wasteland, tripping on some wire, falling, getting up again, taking several steps and then taking a perfect shot in the back of the head.

Ape turned to face me, pistol in his hand.

I said nothing. There was no more to say.

Within a minute, the commander came running, accompanied by several of our men.

'What happened?' he asked, looking at his soldiers, checking no one was wounded or bleeding or had otherwise come to harm.

'He tried to escape…' began Ape.

'Stand to attention,' said the commander, looking directly in Ape's eyes for a moment.

'An ape, that's all you are,' he said, and spat.

I remembered that damp spring night when we were getting ready to leave for Chechnya. We were assigned arms, we assembled grenade launchers, wrapped magazines in insulating tape, packed rucksacks, received supplies, and laughed and smoked a lot.

Ape's wife came at four or five that night, or morning, and stood in the corridor, circles under her eyes.

Seeing her, Gnome disappeared into the changing rooms: he sat there quietly, a little downcast.

Ape went up to his wife. They looked at each other in silence.

Even the rowdiest of the men went quiet when they passed near them.

And I too passed by in silence. The woman acknowledged me with a nod. Then I realised she was pregnant. Not heavily, but it was evident—too late to get rid of it, anyway.

Ape's face was peaceful and far away, as though he'd already traversed the fertile black earth of southern Russia and was now hovering above the mountains, eying his prey. Later, though, he suddenly kneeled and put his ear to her swollen belly. I don't know what he could have heard there, but the moment stuck with me: the corridor full of armed men, dirty iron and foul language under yellow lighting, a pale-faced man listening for an unborn child.

'An ape? Is that all he is?' I asked, approaching the corpse. It looked as though a chunk was bitten out of the back of the head.

Nobody answered my question.

Before going on leave, we had a bit of a party. At the height of the fun, we turned off the lights and Gnome had us in stitches by saying in a high-pitched and astoundingly authentic voice:

'I'm blind! I've gone blind!'

'Father, what's wrong?' replied Ape, playing his part.

'Is that you son?' came Gnome's voice. 'Lead me into the light, my boy. Away from the guffaws of these louts, and into the final sunset.'

Just then the lights went on, revealing Gnome borne up in Ape's arms.

Later, we would remember this scene with sadness.

Two days before flying home, Ape and Gnome were part of a small detachment that went to a remote area in the foothills to bring in a Chechen field commander who'd somehow managed to get captured. They flew out by helicopter with some *Spetsnaz* who were either from Nizhni Tagil or Verkhni Ufalei.

The field commander, his face bashed in by boots and rifle butts, was brought in personally by Ape; to spin out the game the *Spetsnaz* troops—I can't remember what city they were from—stood around the helicopter, their guns pointed in various directions. They enjoyed swaggering about like they were bulletproof. It can happen towards the end of a tour. And Gnome was somewhere nearby, gnashing his teeth.

And that was when they were hit, one maybe from Nizhni Tagil, one maybe from Verkhni Ufalei—brought down together in an instant, hard. Gnome went feral his own special way and stayed hidden in the grass while the bullets flew, and didn't respond to Ape's calls. Ape was back on board the helicopter, its blades spinning in wild desperation to get the hell out of there.

Jumping down, sweating, with no cover and exposed, Ape returned fire, then carried the two injured men back, one on each shoulder. Then he brought in the field commander, who, hearing the gunshots, began to wriggle and to flutter his blood-encrusted eyelashes: he was like a butterfly unable to take flight.

Then Ape went after Gnome. He plucked him out of the grass and carried him in his arms to the helicopter.

Gnome didn't have a scratch on him. The helicopter was trying to take off and his eyes were screwed shut as he tried to figure out where he'd been mortally wounded, though he wasn't hurting anywhere. Then Gnome opened his mouth to tell Ape the good news.

Ape was sitting opposite him in a pool of black liquid, silent, missing an eye. Later it was found that he'd taken another bullet in his leg, and a third right under his arm, where the bulletproof vest gives no protection.

Another spray of bullets had got him in the vest, and probably other organs had suffered from the force of the impact, but no one bothered to check his organs: it was enough that he had managed to run for a stretch without an eye and with a piece of lead lodged in his head.

The two from Nizhni Tagil or Verkhni Ufalei survived. And Gnome got a medal.

We returned home with Ape's immense zinc coffin.

His wife received the coffin with a furious expression and beat the lid so hard with her fists Ape must have blinked his remaining eye, still not getting what had happened.

She stood silently at the funeral, not shedding a single tear, and when the moment came to throw soil on the coffin, she stood frozen holding a clod of red earth. We waited for her, then stepped up with our handfuls of dirt. The soil fell and crumbled apart.

Gnome didn't cry so much as whimper, his shoulders shuddering, his chest was as pitiful as ever, like a birdcage, one emitting a gentle trilling and fluttering of wings.

Ape's wife squeezed the soil so hard in her hand that it fell through her fingers, leaving just the stickiness on her palm.

And she arrived at the *pominki* like that, dirt on her hand.

At first we drank in silence, then we began to talk, after a fashion. I kept looking at Ape's wife, with her stony forehead and hard-set lips. I couldn't help myself; I went over and sat down next to her.

'How are you?' I asked, nodding at her belly.

She said nothing. Then, unexpectedly, she caressed my hand.

'You know,' she said, 'he gave me a venereal disease. I was already pregnant. I couldn't completely cure myself or let myself stay infected. The very day he was killed, it went away completely. I went to the doctor and he examined me—it was as though there had never been anything wrong.'

Within a couple of months, while his widow was having a check-up, Ape's house was broken into. Money was stolen, a lot of it—compensation she'd received. And the car keys were taken and the car stolen from the garage.

The widow called me three days after this happened and asked me to come over.

'Any news?' I asked her.

She shrugged.

'An intuition,' she said, rubbing her enormous belly. 'Let's go, I want to visit someone. A witch. She hasn't received anybody for a long time. She says the truth she tells brings bad fortune. But she owes my father a favour, so she'll see me.'

A witch, for Christ's sake! I thought to myself, but I had to go along. I couldn't refuse a widow.

The door was opened by a welcoming, sunny woman, not particularly old, and not dressed in black and without a scarf—not at all the type I'd imagined: smiling, white teeth, a summer dress, beautiful.

'Tea?' offered the witch.

'Thank you,' I said.

We sat at the table. I ate a couple of sweets. The hot, aromatic tea was served in big round cups.

'Who are you looking for?' asked the witch.

'My house was broken into,' replied the widow. 'They made a clean job of it, not like a stranger would. They didn't have to go searching. They knew where things were kept.'

The witch nodded.

'I've brought a photograph,' said the widow.

She took a photo from her handbag, and I remembered that beautiful Chechen day when we were drinking, and then the light went out, and then went on again, and we posed for a photo, all of us drunk already, crowding together to fit in the picture, jostling like horses.

'That's the one who robbed you,' said the witch, casually, brushing Gnome's face with a beautiful nail.

'See him there?' she said, pausing for a moment. 'The way he's seated, he looks taller than the others. Look. But he's small, isn't he? You don't notice here that he's small. He looks bigger than your husband, widow. He's your husband?' She pointed at Ape. 'He's dead now. But he'll have fine children. Clear-skinned. You'll have twins.'

I sat there stunned—the teaspoon in my hand was shaking.

Gnome had resigned from the unit three weeks before, and hadn't been seen since.

'Let's go around to his place!' I almost shouted, when we were out in the street. I was shaking with rage, ready to kill someone.

The widow shook her head indifferently.

Gnome's house was in the suburbs. It didn't take us long to get there and we found it with its shutters closed and a big lock on the door. The kind of lock you use when you're leaving for a long time, and going far away.

I knocked next door. Yes, they confirmed, they'd gone. All of the them: mother, daughter, and him.

We got in the car. Me, shaking with rage. The widow, calm and silent.

'We should report him,' I said, churning, smoking, and looking at the house with hate, as though considering burning it down. 'Find the bastard, get him thrown behind bars.'

'There's no need.'

'What do you mean, no need?' I shot back.

'It's out of the question. He was Sereozha's friend. I won't have it.'

I started the motor and we drove away. The widow had her hands folded over her vast belly, and was smiling.

YOU'RE THE ONE WE'VE BEEN WAITING FOR

COLIN BARRETT

Sprightly gobshite that I am, *in love with life*, I'm up and dressed an hour before Ma stirs. First I feed the birds out back. I crank open the window above the kitchen sink, tear what's left of the sliced pan into confetti and hoik the pieces into the driveway. The birds come rushing out of the air, out of the dewy folds and pockets of the trees. They strafe the tarmac, cut viciously across one another. There's half a dozen or so of the little brown and grey ones, some with white or black spotted crests, and sometimes one of the bigger black boyos, the crows or whatever, will drop in, though generally they prefer to sit up top the telephone wires and watch the world go by, stirring only to let out a squawk or finick with their bitumen feathers.

When the birds are done I go out back. I start the Hiace and finesse her down to the edge of the drive. I stick her in park and leave the engine running, hoping she'll have worked through her gurgles and wheezes and be purring smoothly by the time we hit the road. I slip back into the kitchen and Ma's up now, knuckling two pills into the hollow of a spoon and stirring them through her coffee, doziness cobwebbing the crinkles round her eyes. I down seven chocolate digestives and slurp through two jet-black mugs of coffee in the time it takes her to get through half a cup of Nescafé. Soon I'm moon-eyed with sugar and caffeine. I get up from the table and do a little tap dance of impatience across the lino as Ma gags herself with her shawl and weathers a coughing fit.

'Come on, Ma, shops'll be busy soon!' I bring my palms beseechingly together.

It's a school day, yes, but it's also Ma's dole, shopping and doctor day, so last night I volunteered to help her. Of course Ma put on a dodgy nose at the idea of me missing school but for all her hemming and hawing she was glad of the company.

I scurry up to the bathroom, take a brisk shit *because don't we all* and get back down to the kitchen just in time to see Ma keel forward in her seat and belt her head off the edge of the Formica. She looks up at me, startled, as a welt begins to bloom above her eyebrow.

I can hear the wet, heavy blink her eyes make.

'I'm ready to go now, Dylan honey.'

The drive is a dream. The Hiace, clear throated, rumbles down Moy Hill. The street is pleasingly empty. Sky is blue and clear, spread out in the windshield. Either side of the street, the tiered rows of terraced houses move like escalators up past us as we make our way into the town centre. Glanbeigh town: the crock of shit at the end of the rainbow. At the convent junction, Micky Devlin, venerable town pisshead, is staggering like a gutshot ballet dancer across the road. He tries to sidestep the arse of a parked Saab but glances the tail light with his hip and is spun off his axis, tottering sideways up onto the pavement and finally coming to rest against the glass facade of the AXO insurance shop. Even for Micky, it's a little early to be that pissed.

'Yup Mick!' I shout out the window.

Micky looks around, sees me, smiles.

'Paddy Carmody's lad!' he roars. His beard looks like one of those tangles of fuzz you pull out of the innards of a hoover.

'I remember him!' he shouts, 'D'you know that!'

I shoot him an acknowledging wave.

'Who's that?' Ma asks.

'He knew Da, apparently,' I say, wanting to leave it at that.

'Must be a man of some distinction, so,' Ma says. She pulls her black glasses out of the tangles of her hair and draws them down over her eyes. The red table mark is still there.

Just before Tesco's I pull off the road. The Hiace mounts the kerb with a hiccup of effort. It's a glorious day, Glanbeigh dressed to the nines in spite of itself, in a flowing fur coat of sunshine. Tatters of rubbish putter in the street like parade bunting. Ma stares mutely out the window, entranced by nothing, or everything. I turn to her and am confronted by two wonky duplicates of my own lovely face, floating in the outer space of her sunglasses.

'Where to Ma?' I chirp.

'What time is it?' she asks, after a long pause.

I make a show of looking at my bare wrist. 'Ten past nine' I say.

'We'll go to Tesco first, then go sign on, then to Dr Birch's,' she says eventually.

'Sound by me,' I say.

'Do you want to go anywhere, honey?' she asks, 'Dunnes or Penneys, get yourself a nice jumper or pair of corduroys for summer?' She gives me a girlish smile, and I can tell she's confecting an airbrushed me in her head, my face spot free and shining with a pristine nancy boy lustre, my hair clean and combed, in a catalogue sweater and spotless chinos, *how handsome* I'd look.

'I'm sound, Ma,' I assure her, consulting the glimmer of the wing mirror and pulling off towards the Tesco car park.

Ma takes her time with the shop. I take a stroll round the car park, hazard a gander inside the other vehicles parked there. It's the usual shite: backrow babyseats, sunglasses daintily folded on dashes, tree-shaped air fresheners dangling from rear-view mirrors. There's a pileen of rubble up at the far end of the car park. I pick up a lump of plaster and weigh it in my hand. I'm a big lad, sixteen going on twenty-five, solid through the middle, with a jaw square like an action hero's (though sometimes smutched by a pimple or scutty patch of stubble) and sporting lovely big dumptrucks for hands,

hands of such size that even I am occasionally moved to flex and waggle one in front of my face, marvelling at its dimensions.

What could these hands do, I wonder?

Gently I place the lump of plaster back on its pile. It fits snugly into its powdery niche at the top of the little pyramid of crap. There's a kind of satisfaction in placing it back there, of *not* skying it as far and hard as I can. The heat is making me dizzy, so I head to the newsagent's across the road and buy a *Star* and a Coke.

By midday we've arrived at Dr Birch's, and Ma has disappeared beyond the clinic's white door to wrangle herself another prescription. I'm parked across the road. I've stretched myself out across the front seats, wedged my feet up on the dash, and am sliding into the lukewarm shallows of a snooze when a knowing, level drawl wafts in through the open window.

'Mr Carmody. Shouldn't you be in school?'

A tall, smooth-headed silhouette leans in.

'Ah, Mr Keene, hello sir—' I drag my feet down from the dash, twist round and upright in the driver seat and, unable to think of anything else to say, resort to barefaced civilities.

'How're you doing, sir? Lovely day isn't it?'

Mr Keene is my chemistry teacher. He's in his twenties, from Dublin. He's a tall lad, but already bald as a porn star's gowl. Tucked under his jacketed arm is a wilted ham roll bodybagged in clingfilm.

'I hope there's a good reason you're sitting in this van rather than in class, Dylan.'

I look across the road, at Birch's door, then back at Keene.

'It's me mam sir, I—' but I can't finish the sentence. My mouth makes helpless little circles, like a gaffed fish's. I can feel my face getting red.

But then Keene's face clouds over and he takes a step back from the Hiace.

'Well. We'll see you tomorrow at any rate then, Dylan, eh? I figure you might be over whatever it is you have today.'

'Expect I'll be right as rain, sir,' I say, grinning sheepishly, running a thumb along the rim of the steering wheel. Keene, satisfied that he's spooked me, saunters off. A few minutes later Ma emerges from Birch's. We'll get home, sort out the shopping bags, then settle down together for *Countdown* and a cup of tea. Brigid Flax doesn't start till seven.

Every Wednesday evening, on the rented first floor above the Glanbeigh DOG AND CAT pet store, Brigid Flax comes to pray. The room in which she prays is uncarpeted, the walls bare but for two big windows facing the street. At the far end of the room there's a stubby second-hand lectern set before thirty or so plastic chairs, into which the punctual and infirm can settle while everyone else crowds in the back or along the walls. Ma's been coming here for the last year and a half. Word is Flax cured an Enniscrone woman's stomach cancer; that she has visions of Christ, of the plagues and suffering yet to be visited on this world. She's not a priest. This is not a church. And yet, every week, between fifty and sixty people show up here to be lead in prayer by Brigid. In fact most also attend regular Sunday Mass like the good *Catlicks* they are. Ma likes to get here early, five to seven at the latest. We'll find her a seat and then I'll go stand at the back for a little bit. I look down at my polished black shoes. When I take her here Ma insists on a measure of dapperdom from me: I'm in a white shirt, black tie and black trousers, swish as a winebar waiter. As everyone files in, their shoes clatter against the bare floorboards like rain; the sound thickens and slows as the room fills up.

A few minutes after seven Brigid Flax is wheeled in. She's in her mid-fifties, diabetic, wheelchair bound. A tartan blanket covers her legs, her feet, shod in plain white plimsolls, stick out at the bottom, and list off at an angle that makes them seem loose, unconnected to her body. She wears the small, round, dark glasses favoured by the blind and chronic migraine sufferers. Prescription job. Her mouth is turned in, lipless. She's accompanied by a runty looking oul fella with a stringy comb-over and talcumed, blotchy forehead—Brendan Hubble. A former hotelier, alcoholic and hardcore Jesus botherer, Hubble is payrolling this whole shindig.

Once Flax is installed behind the lectern and initiates the first run of prayers I'll skip out, intending to make it back in time for the curtain call. I take the Hiace down to the Peacock Hotel and Bar parking lot, park down the back, where the streetlights don't reach. I do occasional nice business with the lads in school on a line of bangers, fireworks, pellet guns; muckshite mickey mouse ordnance, nothing serious, but the kind that gives teenage boys raging horns. I've a border connection, an old FCA colleague of Da's, who kits me out with whatever I require. My mobile blitters in my pocket. It's a text from Tommy Hogue, fifth year like me, general idiot, tonight a customer.

B DERE IN 5 HEAD

SOUND I text back.

Hogue appears on a bicycle, and I watch him do a wobbly, investigative lap of the car park before he spots me and ambles over. He's squinting in the dark. I flick on the dashlight.

'Christ you'd think you were selling kilos of heroin out here, Carmody,' he grins. I spring the boot, unzipper the swollen Slazenger bag slumped there. From beneath a layer of padding—old rags and towels—I yank out a string of bangers and twinkle them in front of his face. Hogue gives a whistle of appreciation.

'How many d'you say you want, then?'

Hogue's elbows press down on the antlers of his racer's handlebars. He rubs his chin.

'Thirty yoyos worth.'

'Blessus,' I say. I count out a dozen then cut the roll with my penknife. I make a show of recounting them, then hand Hogue the umbilicus of incendiaries. 'Careful now with them, Hogey Bear.'

As if adjusting a seatbelt, Hogue tugs at the strap of the rucksack on his back, until the bag's passed under his armpit and round to his front. He unbuckles it and stashes the bangers. I pocket the crumpled notes and wish Hogue well. He stands up on his pedals, leans forward, and drifts toward the car park exit, and I make out the acknowledging chime of his bell as he takes a left into the tarblack night and disappears. I check my phone. I head back to the DOG AND CAT pet store and step back into the crowd. Flax is finishing up. Her last words are 'He is walking among us, even now, already, and he will soon make himself known to the whole world… thank you, God bless, thank you, thank you.'

Then silence. After a moment a couple of people begin to stir, then the general commotion of leavetaking, the mass creaking of chairs as planted arses hoist themselves up. A few of the older and frailer folk lag behind, forming a trembling ring round Flax's seated frame, petitioning her in low voices, some just wanting to lay a hand on her. Ma's always a bit zoned out straight after. I take her by the elbow and guide her out to the Hiace. It's proper dark out now; the streetlights are on, but the one nearest the Hiace is broken, sticking out like a missing tooth in a smile.

'How was it, Ma?'

'Oh it was good, Dylan, she's always good,' Ma says, climbing into the passenger seat.

I drop her home. Ma takes a couple of sleeping pills with warm milk and hits the hay, the pills already kicking in as she moves about her room with the syrupy slowness of a deep-sea diver. 'Light out Dill honey, I'll see you tomorrow,' she says, slipping her sleeping mask over her eyes.

'Night, Ma,' I say, and snake my hand in through her bedroom door to kill the light. On top of wearing a sleeping mask Ma insists on having all the lights in the house off. I knock out the hall light upstairs and then the sitting room lights, lastly the kitchen light. I should be heading to bed but I don't want today to end, really, because tomorrow is school and school is always more heinous after a midweek break. I'm still in my clean shirt and slacks from the Flax meet. I take the housekey from its hook on the sill by the back door and step outside. It's gone eleven. The street is empty, just the arms of the trees moving slowly up and down like seaweed and the yellow streetlights, necks resolutely bent, staring down into their pools of light and refusing to blink. I jog down the hill, my footfalls pocking the silence. The terraced houses, the aprons of shorn yard grass, are like a recurring dream playing through my head one more time, one more time.

Coming down Main Street now—the pubs still bright-eyed, coaxing a last drink out of the midweek customers; in half an hour they'll spit them same folk out the door, like sucked clean cherry pips. I run down Main Road, Exchequer and Oldcastle Street, take a left at the Moy Estate bridge and run along the quays, parallel to the river's threshing arm. The air is sticky. I'm flootered, stop running once the stone wall and tree-lined drive of St Carmichael's, my school, inches into sight. As I pass I make out the buttery rectangle of a lone lit window on the top floor of the principal's residence— old Father Sturgeon must still be up. I imagine him looming above his kitchen sink, taffeta bathrobe cinched round his walrussy frame, gurgling a throatful of altar boy cum, humming jowlily to opera.

The school recedes over my right shoulder as I wander onwards, following the river's curve, and all that water prompts the usual daft fantasies; of shedding this life like a puddle of clothes by the Moy's muddy shore and wading in, submitting my skinny arse to the river's torsions and darknesses. It'd teach you a lesson or two, that river, it'd kill you just to show you what life is like. *Oh hell, oh well.* Up at the next set of traffic lights I spy the entrance to the public park, and suddenly realise that that's where I'd always intended going.

I doddle through the kiddie playground, savouring the emptiness—the swing saddles twisting in the air, the lunar gleam of the sandboxes, the dither of the seesaw, caught perpetually in two minds. I move off into the brush. After a few minutes of walking I make out, in a clearing beyond a patch of bushes, a small light, and two shapes over a fire—one standing, tall and thin, the other hunched over on the ground. I step closer. The guy standing up has his back to me. I see a maroon wool cap sprouting like a cartoon chimney from a bristly skull, a pair of sticky out ears, a T-shirt and orange sleeveless puffa jacket, the lining ripped at the shoulder blades, cottony stuffing coming out in tufts. In one hand he's holding a beercan and a lit cigarette, and along the arm connected to that hand I make out the greenish scales of a tattoo, a stylised oriental dragon. It's Kerbie Martin, and, now that I'm closer, I can see that the figure on the ground is none other than town pisshead Micky Devlin. Micky's steadily moving a beercan up into the drowned kitten of his beard when he sees me.

'Fucking hell,' he gasps. I step suave as a ghost through the wall of branches into the clearing.

Kerbie turns to face me.

'Well,' he says, as if it was exactly me he was expecting, emerging from the bushes in a dress shirt, tie and slacks.

I know him, and wonder if he'll recognise me. Kerbie's a proper headcase, twenty or so now, charged three times and convicted once of assault, apparently no longer allowed under his own mother's roof. Barred from most every pub in Glanbeigh. I know him from school; when I was in first year he was expelled from Carmichael's for socking the jaw off our ex-PE teacher, Mr Golden. He pokes at the fire with a stick. The flames seem to flinch.

'Whoore you now buck?' he says, a hint of a slur in his voice. He might be steamed. He takes a drag on his cigarette.

'Me. No one. Carmody,' I say. I look at Devlin who looks down at the can in his hand.

'What takes you out this way?' he says, turning back to Micky. It's now I notice the black lump above Micky's eye, the dark drip from his eyebrow. Either he's fallen or someone's donated a savage class of a cuff to the side of his head.

'Bedtime wander.' I shrug my shoulders.

Kerbie raises his hand, inspects the kinks of his knuckles. The dragon tattoo starts at the knob of his elbow and extends down his forearm. A wavy band of lime green scales make up the dragon's body, and end in a yellow-eyed head and thin, razor-toothed mouth, from which a forked red tongue protrudes, etched in and around the cords of Kerbie's wrist.

'I saw you today,' Micky says into his can. His voice is dim.

'Shush now,' says Kerbie. He prods Micky's chest softly with the end of the branch.

'I know you lad though don't I? You're a Carmichael's lad aren't ya?'

'Yeah,' I say.

'I've a good memory. You were in first year wern't ya?'

'I'm in fifth now.'

'Ha,' Kerbie says, 'Wonder what that's like.'

He takes a sip from his can, then bends down and snaps another from the half gone sixpack pitched in the dirt next to Micky. He takes a penknife from his pocket, flicks the blade, levers it in under the tab, and pops the can cleanly open.

'There ya go son.' He throws it to me.

I take a gulp. The beer is warm and foamy, with a metally taint to it, like coins.

'Cheers,' I say.

'So Micky knows ya.' Kerbie looks at Micky.

'Micky knows everyone,' I smile.

'And everyone knows Micky,' Kerbie says, slipping the penknife back into his pocket and raising his can in toast.

Micky, head at an angle, shy-like, or maybe just trying to hide his eye injury, raises his can. His head wobbles uncertainly on his neck. He's making noiseless little shapes with his lips. I figure he's concussed on top of being sauced.

'Here,' says Kerbie, bending over to hand Micky his cigarette. Micky takes a drag and hands it back. Kerbie looks at me, and for a second I think he's going to offer me a drag, but he says nothing.

'When I'm at a loose end I kip out here,' Kerbie announces

suddenly, spreading his arms to take in the clearing. 'Turns out this smelly fucker does too.' He prods Micky in the chest again with the stick. Micky bats it away, grunts.

I take another swig.

We all go quiet for a bit.

'Your dad,' Kerbie says eventually. 'That was it. Your oul fella.'

'It's been five years,' I say; and I *am* impressed by Kerbie's recall here, though I'd say most everyone in town can still remember what happened to Paddy Carmody.

'Oh God bless him,' says Micky.

'*Shush now*. Real People! Are trying to have! A conversation!' Kerbie waggles the end of the stick in front of Micky's face. Micky gropes vaguely at it. Kerbie giggles, then turns back to me. 'Don't mind him. I slipped the poor bastard a couple of tabs of acid on the sly. He's cooked.' He giggles, then goes quiet. 'Lost an arm out in Clearfield right?'

The Clearfield refrigerator plant was where my Da worked as a supervisor.

'He didn't lose an arm. Lump a plastic got stuck in the waste machine there. He was tryina clear it out without having to turn the machine off and delay production, whatever. A spindle went into his wrist, dragged his arm into the rollers. Got it crushed up and bled out 'fore the firemen could get to him.'

Kerbie is rocking slowly back and forth on his heels. He shakes his head.

'Silly cunt,' he says, very tenderly. 'Silly cunt.'

'God rest him anyway,' pipes in Micky, still following our conversation, whatever his mental state. Kerbie belches violently, drops his tin, grinds his heel into it and nudges it with his boot into the flames.

'You're a pious cunt for a pisshead, Micky. Easy to be pious when you're tripping your bollocks off.' Kerbie squats down over the fire, level with Micky. He picks a wishbone shaped twig from the grotty shoulder of Micky's coat and places it carefully in the flickering centre of the blaze. We watch the twig flare then wink out, like a comet in the sky.

'Me and the lads used to hit Clearfield a lot in the old days,' Kerbie says. 'At night. Good place for scavenging like, out back, where they keep the fridges on these pallets in open sheds. Three or four of us'd no bother carting a whole fridge back up over the fence. Me bro Ruairi's got a scrambler. Used to hitch the fridge to the back of it with a bit of rope and drag it all round Baleek forest, bumping the shite out of the fridge over all the oul' pathways. And we'd take turns sitting into it, getting the shite bumped out of us too. Mad craic.' Kerbie shakes his head, and I could swear he's getting a touch misty eyed.

He looks back up at me. 'No offence, Carmody, but yer oul fella was a stupid cunt. There was no need really, was there? Just a sloppy mistake.'

I puff out my cheeks, and realise how cold I am, despite the fire. The sweat between my shoulder blades has iced over now, the breeze coming in at it through my shirt.

'Well, he didn't lose it,' I say, taking another gulp of Kerbie's cheaparse knacker beer. 'This beer is shit by the way.'

Kerbie giggles. He's picking at more twigs in the dirt, parsing them out, separating them into little piles, and when he talks, he talks down into the ground.

'Can't fool a connoisseur, Carmody, can I? I bet—bet he was alright though. Best you can ask of an ould lad is he's just not a pure prick.'

'He was alright,' I say.

Something pops in the fire, shooting up a bouquet of sparks. Kerbie fumbles in the pocket of his puffa jacket, takes out a small white sheet of paper.

'Now. Lad. I've a proposition. If you fancy it.'

'That's what you fed Micky,' I say.

Kerbie looks up at me and grins.

'I've a knack. Got it *inside* his can before he opened it.'

'How's that work?'

Kerbie shakes his head, puts a knowing finger to his nose.

'Trade secret. Now. Do you fancy one?' He rotates the white sheet in his hands.

'Well, the thing is. I'm sort of a pioneer. So I'm already out on a limb here,' I say, waggling the can in my hand.

Kerbie hangs his head and goes into a dismayed fit of giggles.

'You'll do, Carmody. You'll do,' he says. 'Fair enough.'

I fake a long-held-in yawn, stretch my arms.

'Might head off meself actually, cheers for the drink though.'

'Sound, sound,' says Kerbie. I put the tin down on the ground carefully, keeping my eyes on him the whole time.

'You'll be missing out though,' he says, 'See, if I can muster the enthusiasm I'm going to gut this fucker, over here—' he points at Micky '—like a fish.'

Micky blinks slowly but otherwise does not react. The cut on his head is beginning to jewel over into a scab. Kerbie leers in close to Mickey's stony face and barks 'Yeah. I'M GOING TO SLICE HIS FUCKING THROAT OPEN AND DUMP HIS WORTHLESS ARSE IN THE MOY,' before he's overcome by a fit of giggles, keeling over backwards onto his bum. He squashes the heel of his hand into his eye, then lets loose a colossal yawn of his own. 'You wouldn't be on for that though, no?'

'I think a sleep might be better, all round. No offence, like,' I say, and step back into the foliage, ready to run if I have to.

'Could be,' Kerbie says, neatly tearing off a square of the white sheet of paper and dabbing it onto his tongue. He sits up straight, stretches his neck to the left, to the right, then closes his eyes. He sticks up a hand, spreads his dirt caked digits, gives a wee wave in my direction, and stays like that—eyes closed, fingers spread and hanging in the air—until I turn tail and bolt for it.

I'm running again, running home, going against the Moy now, and I'm thinking what I always think when I pass the river; of shedding my skin, disappearing into the dark. And I think: well, what if that's already happened? What if, when I get home, I slip in the back door, toe my way up the dark stairs, fingers spidering along the spine of the banister, and step into my room, to find myself already there, tucked snug under the blankets, asleep all this time. The only sound I'll hear will be the peculiar forceful softness of my sleeping self's breaths. A moment will pass, and I'll reach my hand out to touch my face, to make sure I'm really there.

SOME FACTS ABOUT SONORA
DAVID MOHAN

So I'm going to this diner in Jersey to meet this girl who might be my daughter, and this guy pulls out in front of me with no signal.

'Hey buddy,' I shout out the window. 'Learn to fucking drive.'

I park outside the diner and put the radio on because I'm early and I don't want to go in before the time she said. Some smartass is interviewing a guest about the economy. I take out the envelope with the number from the agency and that name I still find so unusual— Stephanie Wald.

My watch reads 3.55. My wife, Claire, is reading to kids in Queens. She volunteers in a day school. At this moment she might be turning the pages of a storybook. I feel a terrible guilt when I think of her. I feel shame.

I turn the radio off and get out of the car. The concrete exhales heat. It feels in the nineties. I push the door to the diner and a nice polar breeze hits me—they've got the air con on full blast. Already, there are stains under my arms so I go and freshen up in the bathroom. I splash water on my neck and forehead. I slick back my hair and grimace. I've got one of those bad comb-overs you can't do nothing about.

I walk out of the bathroom and this guy shows me to a booth beside a window. It's basically what you'd expect a diner to be. Licence plates on the walls. Shiny metal sidings, Home Loan adverts on the placemats. There's a waitress talking to a family in the booth next to mine. The family seem very Midwest to me—wind-blown, too many kids, harried. When they've paid, the waitress walks up to me. She's got a clip with 'Luanne' printed on it.

'You ready to order?' she asks.

'I'm still waiting for someone.'

'Alrighty. I'll do your table.'

She wipes a clean swoop across the table, then another and another, on and on until they all join up and the table is gleaming. This is a nice way to start a conversation, I can't help thinking. I get engrossed watching as she puts down new settings and napkins and cutlery. Everything you might need, all formal, to make an occasion of it.

'Looks like you're set up now,' she says. I feel her shadow shift away.

'What's that?' I say.

When I look up there's this fat woman standing over me.

'Are you George Maitland?' she asks.

'That's right,' I say, standing up. We shake hands. 'You must be Stephanie.'

She sits down with a deep sigh. 'Today is too hot. I can't think, it's so hot.'

As far as I can see, Stephanie is homely, but that's okay. I've seen worse. Better too, but it's honestly okay. She's what you might call frowsy. She's wearing a worn-looking denim jacket, tight pants and too much gold jewellery. Rings all over. She has some hips on her. Too much pie and popcorn, I'd guess. She has a wild splash of freckles on her face.

She leans back and sighs. I sit looking hard at her like some fool trying to work out whether there's some way this woman could be my only child. At first glance she's not my idea of a daughter. Blonde, heavy breasted—she looks like a frizz-haired Veronica Lake.

I get a waft in the cool air of liquor and sweat. I'm no saint myself but I draw the line at morning liquor. She holds still a moment and basks in the air con. Her fingers are nervy—they tremble when she tries to rest them on the table.

Luanne comes back with her notebook open.

'You two know what you want?'

Stephanie picks up the menu and skims through it. 'I'll try pancakes. The Deluxe,' she says. She frowns at Luanne. 'Comes with bacon, don't it?'

Luanne nods.

Stephanie hands her menu back. 'That's the cure for me then.'

I point out my salad. 'This one. Easy on the dressing.'

'And for drinks?' asks Luanne.

'Just water,' I say. 'Bring a carafe.'

'Sure thing.' Luanne takes my menu and stalks off.

She comes back directly with our water and glasses. Stephanie picks up the carafe. 'I'll be your server today,' she says. She pours out two glasses. Her hands shake as she pours and she spills water on the table. Her brow shines with a fresh sweat.

'You drink often before lunch, do you?'

'That's right', she says. 'I do.' She shakes her head. 'Sue me.'

I hold my tongue and sup my water. All the time I can't help wondering how much money this woman wants from me. I look out at the parking lot for a spell and she lays her hands on the table. Her nails are silver-blue, the polish all shot. What am I going to say to this woman? I think. What can I possibly say? In the first place, her mother never let me meet her when she was a kid. In the second, I didn't care that much.

'So, how'd you track me down?' I say.

'An agency,' says Stephanie. 'Almost got killed with documents. There's all this complicated stuff they make you go through. Birth parents guidance and so on. There is actually a bureau called Parent Finders of Waldwick. Couldn't make it up! Mom had some old letters too, of course. You fell out of touch apparently.'

'Something like that,' I say. 'I never heard from your mother in almost two decades. Didn't expect to. Didn't want to. Not a postcard between us for eighteen years. Next I heard she died.' I feel riled up. Perhaps she grew up hearing her mother was a saint, but I knew the whole story.

'That's all I know, anyhow,' says Stephanie. Her eyes swerve off, distracted.

'One Deluxe coming up,' says Luanne, putting the plates on the table.

We start on our food. I eat around the dressing as much as possible and watch as Stephanie tucks away roll after roll of syrupy pancake. She's some sight chewing, her cheeks as big as a woodchuck's.

'You've got to love the Deluxe,' she says. 'I'm on a diet. Pretty much always. But you've got to cut loose sometimes.'

I nod at her and pick over my salad. This girl turning up is not doing my digestion much good. I get queasy when I'm missing sleep, and lately I've been waking early. I lie there and listen to the backyard birds singing. Claire's not much better. I hear her fussing in her bedroom across the hall.

'You work round here?' I say, just to break the awkwardness.

'Sometimes.' She laughs. 'And what about you?' She sips her drink. 'What's your line of business?'

'Real estate.'

'All set up, are you?'

'You know what it's like,' I say. 'Not so good.' I try to look concerned. Earlier today, I sat in my office counting dollars for this woman. I tucked a fat envelope into my shirt pocket. I can feel the shape of it sitting on my rib-cage.

'It's not so easy out there for anyone,' I say.

'That should be on a bumper sticker,' she says, and gives those unruly hands of hers a good scratch. I look away out of politeness on account of those hands being all scabbed over from being picked at.

'The thing is, George,' she says, 'I wanted to talk to you face to face. I've got a request for you.' She spills the contents of her purse onto the table. All kinds of stuff falls out—bunched-up receipts, packets of gum, a plastic dinosaur.

'A girl's life is in her purse,' she says. 'Now, where is that notebook?'

I know what's coming and so I slide the envelope across the table. She stops her rummaging and looks at it.

'What's this?'

'It's something for you,' I say. 'The condition being it's a one-time only payment, and I don't want any trouble in the future.'

She looks at the envelope as though it had landed there from outer space. She shivers then with those flaky hands of hers, and whispers something I don't catch about kindness, and scoops it into her purse. I feel a lightness in my shirt pocket now, a lightness in my chest. I'm keen to pay up and be finished now the money part is over with.

'Can I ask you something, George?' She brushes her hand through her hair with those cut up hands again. 'Aren't you interested in anything after all this time? Don't you want to know what's been going on?'

'Let's face it,' I say. 'I don't know you from Adam. We're talking about almost forty years ago.' I'm feeling a bit worn down by this. What does she expect from me—tears and kisses?

'You sure know how to make a girl feel old, George,' she says. She extracts a notebook from her handbag. 'I've been writing a little family history. It's all for my boy, Scott. Just lately, he's been asking to know more about his dad and about his mom's dad too. It's all stupid kids' stuff, I know, but would you write something for him?'

She slides the notebook across and the page is open on a child's drawing of a big tree drawn in crayon. Silver foil stars light a blue night sky. 'What do you want me to say?' I ask.

'Whatever you want. It's up to you. It's a scrapbook. We stick pictures in it and he writes stuff.'

I can't think of anything. I flick through the pages—they've stuck in poems and postcards and cuttings from magazines. The picture of the tree has names written in for each branch. I start to think about Claire. She would be on the subway by now. She'd be clutching her purse on her knee—it would be bursting with storybooks. Perhaps she'd stop for lunch somewhere and then go home. She likes to lie down in the middle of the day if she can.

'I don't know what to write,' I say.

She takes the notebook back and turns to a new page. 'Look at this now.' She holds up a page with a picture of the desert stuck in. 'We did this page about Scott's dad. We've put in a postcard from New Mexico, some facts about Sonora. Scott drew a picture of a cowboy hat.'

'That's nice,' I say, not knowing what to think.

She turns a page. 'Anyway. The point is that this is what my Scottie likes. Stories. Memories. That kinda stuff.'

I get out my fountain pen, the one I use for checks and business. She passes the notebook back and I open it on a clean page. I can't think of anything at first but then I start writing about when I was a kid. I can remember sitting on the kerb on Florence street in Madison, Wisconsin. I was six years old. I can remember watching the cars go by and thinking how fine it was to be six. I tell this boy, Scott, that I never wanted to be any older. But I grew up and it was fine and everything would be fine for him too in the future. I sign it George Maitland. I hand it back to Stephanie and she reads it to herself.

'I couldn't think of much,' I say, by way of explanation.

'This is good, George,' says Stephanie. 'This is just the thing.'

'You got a photo of the kid?'

'You curious?' she says. 'You don't seem too sure.'

'It doesn't matter,' I say. 'You don't have to show me.' I look out into the parking lot. The sound of the car tyres whizzing down the main street is set to mute. This girl's kid might as well be a Martian as my grandchild, so what do I care about a crummy photo? It's too late for some things and that's that.

She passes her phone across and lit up on the screen is a little blond kid with a toy truck. He's not like anyone I know.

'Satisfied?' asks Stephanie. She sits back in her chair. I tap my wallet on the table top as a sign. I say 'check' when Luanne walks near.

'Prepare to sweat,' says Stephanie.

She puts on her denim jacket and strokes her hand through her hair. We walk to the counter and Stephanie stares out the window while I pay. In the parking lot, she puts on shades and starts to drift off from me as we walk.

'I'll drive you home if you like.'

'You could be a serial killer or something,' she says. She stops walking and stands staring at me. 'You know I'm not supposed to take a lift with you, but go on. I don't usually like to walk round here—it's not so nice along this strip.'

I look at her then—she looks tired. Someone needs to fix her jacket collar but I don't mention it. 'It's no trouble,' I say. We walk to my car.

'That's a nice one,' she says, stroking the top. 'I like the colour. This will do just fine.'

We drive along the state route towards Glenrock. She lives out near Paramus, she says. It's just 10 minutes away. I reckon I have the time. Along the way, I stop at a gas station to buy some cigarettes. I can't help looking back as I pay, thinking that she might fire up the engine and drive off without me. You get those sorts of thoughts sometimes.

She stops me outside a place called Maple Drive apartments. The place is a real dive. The only nice thing is a little park with a playground, just adjacent. The leaves of the maples turn and flash, a bright pale green. The agent in me gets stirred up at the sight of trash cans rolling on the sidewalk

'Wait a while,' she says, 'let me fix my mouth before I step out.' She snaps open her purse and roots out a compact and some lipstick. It is a shocking red, which comes as no surprise. She scrutinises herself thoughtfully. 'My word, look at me—I am a disorderly woman.'

She fixes herself up and then turns to face me.

'If you want to come back sometime and see the kid, it's apartment 16,' she says.

I consider this.

She takes a deep breath and sighs it out. 'My last boyfriend looked just like you. The more I think about it. Isn't that strange?'

I look at her and feel too tired in this heat to say anything.

'I understand,' she says. 'Let's just leave it here. These things get too complicated.'

She places her hand on mine. Up close, her fingers look raw and sunburnt. There is a nasty mark up her wrist I hadn't noticed before.

She sees me look at it and pulls her sleeve down.

She gets out and I drive off. I drive round the block and turn back again. I want to ask her more about that mark. When I drive past the apartment building she's gone, but there's a car parked outside. It's a black Chevy. As I pass I squint at the windows to see if I can see a kid's face, but the glass is tinted.

I drive away then from Paramus. I imagine Stephanie walking into her apartment. Cartoons are playing on the TV—the babysitter is distracted or asleep. She takes off her jacket and soon she hears a soft run of footsteps approaching in the hallway. She stoops down to receive the warmth of a small body into her arms.

I think all of this along Route 17 to the city, and in a short while I am lost in the flow of traffic.

TIGER, TIGER
JULIAN GOUGH

In a church hall on the outskirts of McAlester, Oklahoma, Tiger Woods is helping Trey Carmel to hone his technique. Earlier, before Tiger's arrival, the small, hand-picked crowd had been abuzz with talk of the erupting scandals that have engulfed Tiger Woods, this calm man who has been world famous for fourteen of his thirty-four years. But now they just listen, spellbound. 'Your stance is good,' Tiger is telling the starstruck thirteen year old, 'but you're addressing it all wrong.' The kid nods soberly as Tiger continues; 'I mean, I agree with you, the modernist project has proved to be, in many ways, a dead end. But it's counterproductive to say it flat out. It leaves you nowhere to go. Maybe take a more oblique approach...'

Officially this is Tiger's day off. No writing, no readings. Which means he gets to spend the day in intensive workshops like this one, helping deprived inner city kids become a little better at the thing at which he is a master. He doesn't get paid. The Tiger Woods Foundation costs Tiger an estimated three million dollars a year, not counting loss of earnings. But, for the outsider who's come to dominate the modern novel, for the Great American Novelist with a genetic heritage so rich it qualifies him to enter (and win, five times, so far) the British Commonwealth's Booker Prize, this is an essential part of the working week. 'You've got to put something back,' Tiger tells me later. 'I learned that from my father.'

One momentous day, the two-year-old Tiger Woods astonished

his father, the poet Earl Woods, by climbing down from his high chair, picking up a crayon, and executing a passable imitation of a haiku on the refrigerator door. Earl recalls, 'It was at that moment I realised Tiger had an extraordinary talent that we were going to have to protect and nurture.' When Tiger was still a toddler, Earl says, the child was able to identify the stylistic flaws of adult writers. ('Look, Daddy,' Tiger would say, 'this man is telling, not showing!') Tiger improvised a sonnet with Bob Hope on TV at the age of two, wrote a villanelle at the age of three, and received his first autograph request when he was still too young to do joined up writing.

The day after the McAlester workshop in Oklahoma City (a town not famed for the size of its literary audiences), Tiger Woods draws a crowd of three thousand for a reading that lasted two exhausting, exhilarating hours. His latest novel is at number one in *The New York Times* hardback fiction list. His previous novel is at number one in paperback. And everything else he has ever written drifts lazily about the top 50. In American cultural history, there has been nothing like this since the Beatles. There has been nothing like this in fiction, ever. Where did Tiger Woods come from? Where is Tiger Woods going? And why do we all want to tag along for the ride?

Earl and Kultida Woods both made enormous sacrifices to help Tiger realise his ambitions as a writer. Earl estimates that the family's annual stationery and postage expenses during Tiger's poetry years amounted to as much as $30,000, a sum Earl couldn't have covered without the help of a succession of home-equity loans.

But it paid off. Tiger first outsold his father in poetry when he was eleven. That same summer, he entered thirty-three short story competitions, and won them all. ('That's when I peaked. It's been downhill since.') At fifteen, he turned novelist. That small-press debut, without a single advertising dollar—selling on incredulous word-of-mouth alone—climbed to number one within two months of publication.

John Banville, the Booker Prize-winning Irish novelist, told me recently, 'I've read just about everybody, and I think I can now say that Tiger has written virtually every truly great sentence I've ever read. He simply does things other writers can't do.'

Now Tiger, at 33—his place in the history books secure—faces a new challenge as his carefully guarded private life is opened to scrutiny. But he has faced challenges, and made difficult decisions, before.

Woods' decision in 1997 to rethink his style, taking it apart and tightening it up, seemed to an outsider almost reckless. That process took more than a year, and it coincided with the only relatively dry spell in his career thus far—a period, which ended late in 1999, during which he won only an award or two. Since then, he's won roughly half the awards for which he has been shortlisted.

The process, developed by Woods and his editor Nan A. Talese, included writing thousands upon thousands of practice sentences, enduring countless hours of tedious parsing, and the acquisition and mastery of an entire contemporary 'street' vocabulary. He also worked out, to build up a lower back that had in the past given twinges after marathon sessions at the writing desk. Woods has always loved to practice, and he is a fascinated and deeply analytical observer of his own style. 'He is the best student I ever had,' Nan Talese says.

'People have no idea how many hours I've put into these books,' Woods himself said shortly before his first triumphant, sell-out reading at Madison Square Gardens (during which he demonstrated a new feminine interior voice, in a rich, Jamaican-Irish patois, which he had developed especially for the unique conditions of the British Booker Prize). 'My dad always told me that there are no short cuts.'

The conventional wisdom among critics used to be that the American novel had become so deep in talent that no modern novelist could hope to dominate it the way Mark Twain or Henry James once did. Now, though, Woods becomes the favourite for any award simply by making the longlist. For the past decade, professional writers all over the world have had to increase their vocabulary, sharpen up their modern cultural references, do sit-ups and abandon beer, in the hope of becoming good enough to be considered second best. 'He's in their heads,' the critic James Wood (no relation) told me.

Nicholson Baker nods sombre assent. 'Look at what's happened to American literature since Tiger exploded on the scene. The strain of trying to keep up with Tiger is literally killing us. Updike. Mailer. Vonnegut. David Foster Wallace...' Baker trails off, and opens his hands in a helpless gesture. 'I mean, I know how they felt! My psoriasis has exploded in parallel with Tiger's rise. We're all running scared.'

James Wood recalls the corrective eye-surgery that Tiger underwent some years ago. 'The first thing he said afterwards was, "Hey, the keyboard looks bigger." Now, if you're Jonathan Safran Foer, is that what you want to hear?'

But Dave Eggers, founder of the literary magazine *McSweeney's*, and author of *A Heartbreaking Work of Staggering Genius*, likes to see Tiger's rise as a positive force for all American writers. 'Look, without him, I might not have even got published. The guy invented the middle-class misery memoir. Who saw that one coming? He's a phenomenon. After he reinvented chick lit, we were all asking ourselves the same question—how does he get into the heads of so many different women? OK, I mean, now we know, but... Tiger has opened up new territories for all of us lesser writers to explore.'

No one has ever dominated the novel as Tiger Woods does. Winning one of the major awards was something writers achieved once, twice, maybe three times in a career. But Tiger has already won the Pulitzer, the Booker, the National Book Award. Five times. Each.

Woods has also changed the literary novel's public image, which has suffered for decades from the art form's suburban association with cardigans, scotch, and manual typewriters. Middle-aged weekend scribblers now stand a little taller at cocktail parties because Woods, miracle of miracles, has made writing seem kind of cool. When a teenage checkout girl at my local grocery store discovered that I did a lot of writing, her eyes lit up and she asked, 'Have you met Tiger?' Woods has even taken the most shameful aspect of the novel's long history—its legacy as a decadent pastime for white people with too much time on their hands—and turned it inside out.

White writers tend to underestimate the emotional impact that Woods' racial background has had on non-Caucasians. Tiger Woods, like Muhammad Ali before him, brings the message: If I can be the best in the world, despite all the odds stacked against me, what could my brothers not do, given the breaks, the chance?

Certainly, Tiger Woods has brought a new constituency to the literary novel. It is a not uncommon sight in these post-Tiger times to see young African-American teenagers arguing fiercely about Dostoevsky or Don DeLillo in the public parks and, increasingly, the public libraries. But mainly they talk about, and they read, Tiger, Tiger, Tiger. Even in the trailer-parks of the South, among the disenfranchised white youth of America, with Eminem blasting from the open windows, it is likely to be a Tiger Woods sticking out casually from the open flap pocket on the hip of the outsize cargo pants.

'Tiger has brought glamour back to the novel,' says Tom Wolfe. 'It was deeply unhip, it was white, it was middle class. Realistically, in a multicultural America where English isn't even going to be the majority language in another few years, it was dying. Tiger saved the novel's metaphorical ass. Tiger made it cool to pick up a book, to pick up a pen.'

If a kid in Compton or Watts does pick up a pen today, it's likely as not to be a Nike Inkmaster. But the various controversies surrounding Tiger's commercial endorsements have more than once threatened to become the story, overshadowing his achievements on the page. The recent revelation that Nike made much of their ink from the spleens of day-old puppies may have tarnished Tiger, who also refused to condemn the mass slaughter and skinning of Chinese orphans in the manufacture of Nike Writing Gloves.

(Slogan: *Hardwearing as Hemingway's hide. Yet soft as a baby's behind.*)
Nicholson Baker dismisses both the controversy and the product.
'Personally, I don't think wearing a pair of Nike Writing Gloves, or
a Nike Editor's Cap, will make you a better writer or a better editor.
Although, heck, I wear a Nike Air-Ed myself. Great soft, inflatable
headband, very light polyvinyl, but with micropores, so the skin can
breathe. The classic green brim filters out UV as well, so you can
edit on your porch if you like, or in the park in the sunshine. I see a
lot of kids doing rewrites in the parks now, working on their second
drafts. And that can only be a good thing.'

Some of the more excitable cultural commentators have said
that Tiger is unique, a freak, of a type never seen before. Tom Wolfe
demurs. 'In many respects he's an old-fashioned writer. He writes
longhand, he types it up on an old Mac. But he happens to be a
natural who has honed every aspect of his technique, ironed out
every flaw. He tended to fade at the finish. So, he worked on it. Now,
when's the last time you saw him fade? His finishing's incredible.
And his mastery of readings... well, he's the best since Dickens.
Nobody can read like him. His delivery is astonishing. The power,
the accuracy...'

Of course, readings killed Dickens, who ruined his health on
lengthy and exhausting reading tours. The American circuit in
particular is probably the most demanding on earth. But Woods
learned from Dickens and didn't make the same mistakes. New
technology has helped too. Dickens had to project unaided to the
back of the hall. Woods uses a light, alloy radio-microphone and
state-of-the-art public address systems, which can project huge
distances with no drop-off.

His emotional range, too, is huge. Norman Mailer, a giant himself
in his day, was gracious in his praise for the man who did most to
erase him from the record books. In Mailer's final interview before
his death, he acknowledged 'Nobody has an emotional range like
Tiger. A lot of these young fellows pitch very high, but their range
is poor. Tiger, Tiger goes for everything. Everything! He has balls,

and he knows what they are for. Nothing is out of bounds for him.' Mailer smiled. 'I like Tiger. Tiger is fearless.'

He will need all his fearlessness in the coming months, and years. If there is anything on earth more ravenous than a Tiger, it is the public appetite for the private lives of celebrities. Now the public have tasted blood—Tiger's blood—and Tiger Woods, the most private of men, finds himself in a fight to master the one story he cannot control—the story of his life.

As I leave Oklahoma City behind me, a line of Tiger's, spoken in a different context, won't stop echoing in my head. Am I wrong in thinking that this master of subtext may well have been referring obliquely to his own talent—and the hazards of fame into which it has led him—when he said to Trey Carmel, with a strange trace of sadness in his voice, 'It leaves you nowhere to go'?

THE YELLOW HANDBAG
CHRISTINE DWYER HICKEY

Under the trees at the edge of the Green, Ashok waits in the car—a Mercedes E-Class Saloon. He is parked in his usual place but this is not his usual car and, like a poor man who has borrowed an expensive suit, he can't seem to get comfortable in it.

Bumper to bumper. Every day it is getting more difficult to find a suitable space. He worries that one of these mornings he will arrive to see double yellow lines, or worse a sign that says 'Resident Permit Only'. And he is no longer a resident here—he is no longer a resident anywhere.

His car is his home. Like a snail, he moves with it. Not, of course, this Mercedes E-Class Saloon, which is only for today's job on the side, courtesy of Burke's De Luxe Chauffeuring. But his own, much more modest, yet no less appreciated, four-year-old silver Mondeo.

It is not the worst arrangement, for a neat sort of fellow such as he, brought up to live in tight spaces. And it has the advantage of being wholly private, unlike the bustee in Bombay, where a game of street cricket was often the only occasion when a chap got to stretch out his legs.

There are many advantages to his self-contained lifestyle—the freedom to sleep wherever he likes, being one. Although the Phoenix Park, with its variety of spaces, would always be his preferred location. But there are certain drawbacks too. Having 'no satisfactory place of residence for Sarla's visits'—to quote from his solicitor's letter of the 14th *ult*. He could not seem to get it into his solicitor's fat head the advantages of a Mondeo over the stinking hole on the North Circular Road, where it had been his misfortune to share with three low-life, hard-drinking, foul-mouthed reprobates. The air festered with the smell of cigarettes, alcohol and farts, the walls covered with posters of bare-tittied women. If he himself had been unable to endure these living conditions, how on earth could he expect his twelve-year-old daughter to spend time in such an environment?

Number two drawback is this—if the Mondeo is his home, it is also the place of his everyday work, that is, his taxi-cab. He thinks now of the priest he picked up at Heuston Station yesterday in a drizzle of morning rain, the way he had rolled down the window and covered his mouth with his hand, causing Ashok to worry then, as he is still worrying now, that despite his best efforts, his Mondeo is beginning to stink.

Ten minutes and a few seconds more. Then Sarla. After that, his airport pick-up. Ashok lifts the information sheet from the passenger seat and checks the details. Flight DL102 arriving 9.45. Passenger Mr J.P. Ridell. He has no idea what to expect from his passenger except that he will be a VIP. Someone who will know not only how to receive respect but also how to give it. A man inclined to conversation, which makes a pleasant change from the usual snatchy chats of the shorter fares about Dublin where Ashok is as likely to get a sneer as a tip. Or worse a babble of drunken nonsense. Riffy-raff types, as his uncle Ravi would say. A day with a VIP is almost always a pleasure. This is particularly true of the longer drives when, after a few shared hours in an intimate space, tongues loosen and hearts relax. At the end of such days it is not unusual for Ashok to be able to say—either to himself, or occasionally someone else: 'Yes, in my line of business I meet some very interesting people indeed.'

Five minutes more. He will see her. He tells himself that this is all that matters. He may not, indeed should not, speak to her, but that is acceptable also. Seeing is believing. And should somebody ask him—as Burke, with his face the colour and texture of naan bread, did only this morning when he came to collect the Mercedes—'So tell us, do you get to see your daughter at all these days?'—he will be able to say in all truth, 'Oh yes, I see her each day before school, without fail.'

He looks out the car window, down the road to the house that used to be his, reaches into his pocket and pulls out a fistful: a miniature four-headed Brahma, a tiny bunch of plastic red chillies and finally Lord Ganesha himself. Looping them through the stalk of the rear-view mirror, Ashok watches them turn, then settle. He stretches his fingers, pressing the palms of his hands together and bows his head over the steering wheel. He prays that he may see Sarla. That he may make a good tip today to put towards her birthday surprise. He prays that he may have peace in his mind, heart and hands.

Sarla! She comes out of the house and lifts her face to the morning. Such a beautiful child, Ashok feels almost in awe of her. Even since yesterday, he sees changes that he can't quite name. And yet there is so very much about his daughter—hair, teeth, eyes, skin—that is undeniably Indian, and therefore undeniably his.

She stands for a moment, blinking at the light, and he knows the word 'sundust' is rising in her mind—a word that he gave her a long time ago. He watches as she balances her schoolbag on the narrow wall and begins fiddling with its strap, her eye, at the same time, trawling for a taxi sign along with the familiar silver of his Mondeo. She will presume he hasn't turned up today. He knows that this will make her at once relieved and disappointed. He feels his heart crack with the weight and pain of his love.

The car slips away from the kerb and prowls around the corner, only whispering to a stop a yard or so behind Sarla. Ashok sits still. He watches as his daughter, turning to cross over the road, glances at the car, glances again. She stops, then takes a third, longer look, over the rise of the bonnet, up the front windscreen, past Ganesha and Brahma, the bunch of dangling chillies, straight into her father's eyes.

She returns to the pavement and comes around to the passenger door, hugging her schoolbag to her chest. Ashok finds the right button and in a moment the glass from the window has dissolved. He leans through it and shouts, 'Hi there, Sarla!', as if it's the biggest surprise in the world to find her here.

Her eyes shift from side to side.

He continues, 'So how are you today? And more to the point, how do you like my new car? Of course it's not really mine, only joking—well it is mine, I didn't steal it or anything, but it's just for today, work, you know.'

He waits but she says nothing. 'Oh Sarla, you are like a picture there, in the frame of the window,' he says, drawing a square with his finger. 'You are truly more beautiful every day.'

'You're not supposed to be here, Dad,' she says. 'You'll get in big trouble.'

Ashok tries a shrug. 'I know,' he says, and then gives a small laugh. 'You won't tell on your old Papa-ji. Eh?'

'I'll be late for school. I better, you know.' She begins moving away.

'But Sarla, I just need to tell you—things are really, really changing fast. You will not believe how much.' He lifts one hand and rolls his eyes in amazement, then laughs again. 'You will see, oh you will see.'

Sarla looks away from him. 'Listen, I really have to—'

'Of course, but first just let me quickly show you something.' He reaches into his inside pocket. 'I shouldn't be doing this, I really should not, but what the hell! This was to be for your birthday—The Ultimate Birthday Surprise! See, it says so, here on the envelope. And I shouldn't say anything until all is settled with your mother, but—'

'Dad, please.'

He pulls two airline tickets out of the envelope and flaps them at her.

'What's that?'

'Only your ticket to India, your Highness. That's right, Sarla, your father is taking you to India. To see your grandmother in Bombay. Or Mumbai as I suppose we must now call it. And all your relatives, so many cousins! All dying to meet the famous Sarla. Is it not truly the Ultimate Birthday Surprise? Can you imagine any better? You see—your father does keep his promises after all? Isn't it true? Say it is so.'

Sarla says nothing.

'I can see you are shocked,' he continues. 'Naturally you are, it is not every day that such a gift arrives. Now, I don't want you to worry about your mother. How can she in all honesty refuse her child this opportunity? I mean what sort of a mother would she be? Six weeks, Sarla, and during the school holidays, so there can be no objection on educational grounds. I have been the greatest of misers, you know, first the tickets, and now I am working on our spending fund. And we don't have to stay in Bombay. Oh no, we can travel elsewhere, India is such a… such a vastness, you know. If you like, we needn't ever come back—oh no, no, only joking. We will come back, of course.'

Sarla bites down on her lip. 'I thought you were supposed to be saving for a new apartment?' she says.

He snorts out a laugh, 'Oh now, such an old head on young shoulders! All that will come. But your poor old Naani, she does not have all that much future left.'

He pushes the tickets towards her. 'Look now! Look! There is your name written just there. Oh and listen, I am finding a new lawyer. A better one. More expensive but, you know, you pay for what you get in this life, Sarla. Here, take a little peek…'

She looks to the sky and her eyes blister with tears.

'What is it, Sarla? Tell me.'

'I don't want to—' she says, 'I'm sorry, Dad. I just can't.'

'You don't want to what?'

'I don't want to go to India!' she cries.

Then she is gone.

He nearly misses his VIP. His concentration wavering on and off Sarla; the traffic so dense, the parking elusive—every time he approaches what he believes to be a free space, he finds some little bastard Mini or Fiat cowering at the back of it. What with one thing and another and all excuses aside, he leaves the bloody 'Welcome Mr J.P. Ridell to Dublin' sign in the car. To make matters worse, he finds he has also forgotten his mobile phone. He glances at the monitor. Already landed.

Ashok watches the arrivals stream through the automated glass doors. His eyes frisk the crowd, dismissing women holding layers of Manhattan shopping bags, young men humped under knapsacks, a fat, red-faced family stuffed into Disneyland jerseys, an old lady carrying a yellow handbag. He keeps his sights only on potential VIP material. If he is looking for Mr Ridell, then Ridell is also searching for him. They will know each other. He is certain of it.

The VIPs begin to stand out; a tall man with a pale mackintosh crooked overarm; a woman in a pinstripe suit, a man dressed in the corduroy, roll-neck, hush-puppie uniform of the American academic; all of whom pause as they come to the barrier and cast about for their names. Ashok is hopeful that he will be chosen but one by one, each VIP locates his driver and disappears leaving only the usual humdrummerie behind: *Welcome to Dublin. Enjoy your flight? Thank you, I did. If you just come this way? Thank you, I will.*

Then the next lot of drivers and greeters begin to arrive.

He puts his chauffeur hat on his head. Despite having given up all hope of Ridell, he continues to stare at the gate. After a while, he removes the hat, tucks it under his arm and makes his way to the customer desk.

'Looking for Ridell?' a voice says somewhere, pronouncing it 'Riddle'. Ashok starts, then turns round. An old woman with a square yellow handbag is standing looking up at him.

'That is quite correct. I'm waiting for Mr J.P. Rid-ell,' he says somewhat stiffly, while at the same time taking the precaution of making a slight adjustment to the pronunciation.

'You're in for a long wait—he's been dead twenty years.'

Ashok blinks and says 'Oh. I am so very sorry.'

'I guess I'm about over it now,' the woman replies. 'I'm Mrs Ridell. Mrs J.P.'

He continues to stare. She has thick coiffed hair, stiff and white as meringue. Her face is beaky, eyes bright and a turquoise sort of blue. She is small and rather slight, yet still capable of carrying her well-cut clothes. Her hand, through the loop of her yellow handbag, is thin and freckled, her nails, manicured and pearly-pink.

'Why yes. Yes of course,' he hears himself blurt. 'You are Missus, not Mister—they have made a mistake at the office. I am so very sorry. Welcome to Dublin,' he adds, diving straight into the pleasantries. 'I hope you had an enjoyable flight. First time here? The weather has been most—'

'You don't have a sign. I'm supposed to look for a sign?'

'Yes, Ma'am. I do apologise. But if you care to tell me where your luggage—'

'Got any ID?' she asks him then.

'Ma'am?'

'Something to prove you're my chauffeur?'

Ashok waits a moment before sheepishly taking his hat from under his arm. 'I have a hat,' he offers.

'He has a hat,' the woman repeats. 'You know, anyone can have one of those? Oh what the heck,' she decides after a moment, 'what's the worst he can do—strangle me?'

'Really Madam,' Ashok begins to protest, but already she is trotting ahead of him towards the exit door.

'My stuff is over here. I need to smoke. Now why don't you show me where I can do that while you go get the car?'

Back at the Mercedes, he checks his mobile phone. One message received. 'Sarla!' he says, 'Sarla. I knew you would come round.' But the message turns out to be from Burke.

Got him yet?

He pulls the trinkets and gods from the rear-view mirror and stuffs them back into his pocket. '*Her*,' he then snaps at the phone. 'It's a bloody woman, you dough-faced fool.'

He settles Mrs Ridell into the back of the car, then twists in his seat to show her the Welcome Mr Ridell sign. 'You see Ma'am—how it says here Mister? But see now—' Ashok takes a pen from his pocket and carefully writes the letter S beside the Mr.

He holds out the sign. 'Now we are all clear. I know who you are, and you know who I am.'

'Right,' she says, settling into the seat, 'so. You know a house by the name of Farmleigh?'

'If you mean the large house by the Phoenix Park, Ma'am? Then I do, only last week in fact I took a government minister to—'

'Good. So you can take me there now. And if we could drive through the Phoenix Park? Oh, and I'd like to go via the Four Courts, if you don't mind.'

'Would you care to go now, Ma'am, or would you prefer to go first to your hotel to freshen up?'

'Do I look as if I need freshening up?'

'Oh no, Ma'am. You look quite fresh enough already.'

She raises her eyelids.

'What I mean to say, Ma'am, is not that you look fresh but—'

'So I don't look fresh enough?'

'Oh you do, Ma'am, but—'

'So how do I look then? Go ahead, be honest, say the first thing that comes into your head.'

Ashok can hear the gulp in his throat.

'Like a lady, Ma'am.'

'Like a lady, he says,' Mrs Ridell laughs and sits back into her seat. 'I'm sorry—what's your name again?'

'Ashok.'

'I'm sorry, Ashok, I'm just kidding.'

'That's quite alright, Ma'am. I too, enjoy a little joke from time to time.'

They leave the airport and in the mirror he sees Mrs Ridell fussing through various items in her square yellow handbag. She looks like a child back there, so small and well-behaved, surrounded by a big bank of leather. Like Sarla once was. Except Mrs Ridell isn't a child. She is a small adult with an old face. And a big yellow handbag.

He wonders what to do with her now. To make conversation or wait to be spoken to? To run through the itinerary or await instructions? Or to throw a few 'touristy snippets' over his shoulder, as Burke has advised him to do in times of tight silences. But the silence is not tight, and Mrs Ridell seems most content to continue playing with her handbag. He thinks of Uncle Ravi, for years a driver for a tour company in Rajastan until an incident—never to be spoken of—got him the sack. 'Lady People,' is how Ravi referred to passengers such as Mrs Ridell. 'They are a different breed altogether, they need more attention. You must address them often, and always as Ma'am. And, above all else, you must constantly be on the check to see if they are comfortable.'

The car drives down through the redbrick and foliage slope of the Drumcondra Road when he notices Mrs Ridell lift her small head to look out the window.

'Ma'am?' he asks.

'Yes, Ashok?'

'Comfortable, Ma'am?'

'Thank you I am—how about yourself?'

'Myself—Ma'am?'

'That's right.'

'Oh! I'm comfortable also.'

He glances at the car clock. Three minutes to eleven. Soon Sarla will be on her morning break and will likely give him a call. He wonders should he perhaps mention it in advance to his VIP? He considers how to put it. 'My daughter, you know, we had a little misunderstanding this morning. I hope you don't mind if I take that call? Children at that age, you know how it is? She has just entered her teens and I don't want her upset all day long.'

He draws up at the traffic lights and is about to speak when Mrs Ridell's little frosted head pops between the front seats. She is holding a page between her pearly nails. 'The itinerary—if you care to look it over?'

Ashok glances down through the list before the lights change again. The Phoenix Park remains in his head; the American Ambassador's residence; Myo's pub; Farmleigh House and something about a racecourse. The next set of lights and he stops again, taking a glance at the end of the list where he reads the Bailey pub and, finally, the Shelbourne Hotel for 7.30.

He looks at his mobile phone, then back at the clock. Ten minutes past. In five minutes Sarla's morning break will be over. Perhaps he should call her instead?

'You see, Ashok,' Mrs Ridell says, 'I reckon I'll be about ready to sleep by eight-thirty this evening. I go to bed most nights by nine thirty anyhow. So I thought—why not put in the day with a ride down Memory Lane?'

'Oh yes, Ma'am. It's a lane we all must ride down from time to time.'

The clock passes the quarter mark. 'Comfortable, Ma'am?' Ashok asks.

'No change there, Ashok.'

They cross Capel Street bridge and turn up Essex Quay, a soft drift of river air through the half-opened window. Across the way, the Four Courts, solid and sunlit behind a fluster of leaves from the trees at Arran Quay wall. 'Where's the stink gone?' she asks and Ashok feels a moment of alarm.

'The stink, Ma'am?'

'You know—the stink? This river used to stink to high heaven.'

'Oh that stink, Ma'am. Well—I don't really know.'

Mrs Ridell edges over to the quayside window. She opens it fully.

'Would you care to get out for a moment, Ma'am? If you have a camera I could take a nice snap of you?' Ashok asks as he pulls the car into a space by the river wall.

But she already has a packet of photographs in her hand. He watches a blur of black and white images slip behind each other, until one is finally chosen. It is an old photograph of the Four Courts. Mrs Ridell, her head dipping up and down, from the photo to the subject, appears to be verifying something or perhaps Ashok thinks, even looking for changes.

'Alright, thank you. Drive on,' she says with an absent-minded pat of her hand on the back of his seat, and he knows then she is used to having a chauffeur.

Ashok turns the nose of the car into the Phoenix Park. On Chesterfield Avenue he says, 'Ma'am, you will notice here the tearooms. Over there the cricket ground, in a moment the polo grounds. It is not unlike India in this respect. The colonial connection, of course, and—'

'Yes, that's fine,' she says.

He decides to abandon the touristy snippets.

At the Ambassador's residence, Ashok helps her out of the car and watches her move towards the entrance gate. Once more, she begins to sift through her photographs. She turns to him then, waves and points to her wristwatch to indicate that she won't be long. He sits back into the car, waits for her to disappear around the side of the Ambassador's residence before picking up his mobile and sending a message to Sarla. She will be in class, but he knows these little scamps, they are always sending texts to each other, never minding the rules.

Sarla hope u better mood? x Dad

He puts the message through, checks the report that says it's been delivered, and waits. Through the mirror his eye falls on the yellow handbag in the back seat of the car.

Mrs Ridell is gone so long Ashok begins to worry. He gets out of the car and looks around. Then he walks to the tunnel of trees that runs alongside Chesterfield Avenue and peers down into its maw. He sees walkers, joggers, a dog zigzaggedly sniffing, a woman walking like an overwrought puppet. And a little girl on a tricycle, a man trotting behind her—a sight which seems to squeeze on his heart.

He gets back into the car and sends another message to Sarla.

Sarla plse ans. all is ok to your father.

The report states the message is pending. Ashok can hardly believe it—has she turned off her mobile phone? He calls the number and is put straight to message minder.

His first reaction is anger. She is cutting him, just like her mother has done so many times in the past. Switching off the phone. Locking all doors. After all the penny-pinching and doing without. All the looking forward to—no more than that—all the living for the moment when he would hand her those airline tickets. And look how she had reacted to those! And now this cold-shouldering—is this how he is to be repaid for all his love and hard work!

OK. b that way. U will b sorry now. Am finished with you. Forever.

Ashok looks at the text he has written and feels a small tingle of satisfaction. He continues: *Jus like yr bloody mother.*

He feels better again and adds: *yr bloody whore mother. Selfish bitch.*

U prob not even mine. I wasn't the only Indian driver in that cab company when she worked on the switchboard!!!

He immediately regrets and is ashamed of his message, even if he never had any intention of sending it. Poor little Sarla. After all, she is just a child. Also it is quite possible that her teacher has confiscated the phone. Sarla would never be so cruel as to ignore him. He lifts his finger to the delete button, but a rap on the back window startles him and when he looks at the phone again he sees 'message sent' gliding across the screen. 'Oh no,' he groans, 'what have I done? I have pressed the wrong bugger.'

He jumps out of the car and opens the door for Mrs Ridell.

'You say something?' she asks him.

'Oh no, Ma'am. Nothing, I said nothing.'

Ashok's hands feel slightly weak, as he gets back into the driver's seat. He clutches the rim of the steering wheel. 'Comfortable, Ma'am?' he says.

'Look, why don't we agree on something? When I'm no longer comfortable, I'll let you know—okay?'

'Yes, Ma'am,' Ashok says.

'Anyhow. Let's try for Farmleigh.'

'Oh yes, Ma'am. In fact only last week I took a government—'

'So you said.'

The gates of Farmleigh are firmly shut. Mrs Ridell stands with her nose to the bars. There are strings of wet grass and muck on the heels of her shoes, Ashok notices. The security guard tells her, then tells her again. The house is closed to the public except for certain days and this is not one of them. He is a fat chap, his belly pushing against the blue of his shirt. Mrs Ridell will not be told: 'But I just need to see it. I won't take more than ten minutes, tops. Okay, five. Five little minutes.'

'I'm sorry. I just can't.' He looks over her head at Ashok. 'I can't,' he shrugs and gives an apologetic grimace.

'What are you telling him for?' Mrs Ridell says. 'He's just the driver.'

Ashok, returning the grimace, smiles broadly at the security man. 'Just the driver,' he confirms.

'Oh come on now,' Mrs Ridell says, 'surely you can help me out here? What difference is it going to make to your life? Five lousy minutes. Am I being unreasonable here? Am I asking too much? An old woman at the end of her days?' She draws her hand around in a semi-circle as if appealing to a jury only she can see.

'Sorry,' the security guard says.

She speaks to Ashok from the side of her mouth. 'Could you bring my purse from the car please?'

Ashok returns with the bag.

'I can pay you for your trouble,' Mrs Ridell says to the security man, snapping her fingers at the bag as though beckoning it. 'I mean if it comes to that.' Ashok steps forward and holds the bag out to her. But Mrs Ridell doesn't take it. Instead, she shoves her two thin arms through the rails of the gate, pulls one photograph out of her bundle and thrusts it at the security guard.

'I was a guest here a long time ago. See? That's me. Right there.'

Ashok stretches his neck to see the frame of a large house, people sitting outside it, a conservatory, a lawn. He can't see the woman who used to be Mrs Ridell because the pink-pearly nail of the present Mrs Ridell, is blocking his view. The security guard won't look at the picture. He backs away, raising his hands as if he is expecting Mrs Ridell to draw out a gun. 'Lookit. Even if I wanted to, I couldn't. There's an important meeting on. Government biz, you know yourself.'

'You know yourself? You know yourself?' Mrs Ridell asks, 'What in hell's that supposed to mean?'

'Sorry now.'

He walks away up the avenue. She stands for a while looking after him, the fan of photographs still in her hand. Ashok stands beside her, the yellow handbag looped over his arm.

Mrs Ridell gets back into the car. Ashok cautiously places the handbag beside her.

'Oh how disappointing,' she says looking out the far window, 'how very, very disappointing.'

'I am sorry Ma'am, I thought you were aware it was no longer a private house.'

'Oh, for goodness sake, how could I know that!'

He is about to drive off when the mobile sounds, then sounds again. He checks and sees both his messages to Sarla have just gone through.

'Ma'am?' he begins, turning to look over the back seat, 'I wonder, Ma'am, if I might take a moment to send a message on my mobile, I mean my cell telephone? It is a matter of urg—'

'Oh go ahead,' Mrs Ridell says with some impatience.

Sarla—so v. sorry for last message. Sent in error. Please forgive. Love from so sorry dad.

'So,' Mrs Ridell sighs, 'the racecourse, I guess.'

'The racecourse, Ma'am?'

'That's right. The Phoenix Park Racecourse. Tell you what, let's see if I can remember how to find it.'

'Yes, Ma'm.' Ashok says and begins following her directions.

They go back into the Park where, just before Ashtown Gate, she asks him to pull to the kerb.

'Ah yes, Ma'am,' he says. 'I understand now. But you do realise—?'

She has the door open and is half out of the car before he has a chance to tell her. Ashok slips his mobile phone into his pocket and hurries around to help her. They pass through Ashtown gate onto Blackhorse Avenue and Mrs Ridell says, 'Oh my! Oh no!'

He helps her to cross the road, holding her at the elbow and, with his other hand, gestures a car that has come spinning around the corner too fast.

They stand at the entrance of the former racecourse, the ground at their feet mutilated by heavy machinery, the air muffled with the churn and rattle of a building site.

'I never thought,' she says, raising her voice to carry, 'I mean, of all the—you know? The last thing I expected in Ireland, in Dublin, was to find a racecourse well, obliterated, I guess. And for this? What is this anyhow?'

'Apartment-living, I believe they call it, Ma'am. Or something.'

'Or something, he says!' She gives him a look of disgust in return for his inadequate explanation.

As they cross back over the road, Ashok's phone, like a large bee in his pocket, buzzes.

'Oh please—don't mind me! You go on right ahead and take it.'

He pulls the phone out of his pocket and turning one shoulder slightly, reads a message from Sarla.

If u don't leav me alone. I tell u been following me. I tell Mam and she call police. BTW I hope NOT yrs cos I rly rly HATE u.

'Everything okay?' Mrs Ridell asks

'Oh absolutely perfectly so, Ma'am. Thank you for asking,' Ashok replies with a cheek-splitting smile.

'You know what I could do with?' Mrs Ridell says, when they get back to the car. 'I could do with a drink, is what.'

Mrs Ridell comes out of Myo's, two bindi-like spots high on her cheekbones. Ashok takes her elbow and guides her in, closing the door on a dark yeasty waft of over-ripe figs. In other words, whiskey.

'So—you get to finish making all your calls?' she asks.

'Excuse me, Ma'am?'

'I was by the window. And came out for a cigarette—you were on the cell phone, like, the whole time.'

'It was only the one call and I couldn't get through. The person is no longer in range.'

He turns and looks over the seat at his VIP. She is tidying the photos away, returning them to the flap, then into a zip compartment of her handbag. She now begins working on the rest of her items, which are still spread all over the back seat: pen, cosmestic-bag, compact mirror, hairbrush, three or four boxes of pills. Ashok finds it astonishing that so few possessions could take up so much space. She glances at him, eyes dull, skin a little faded, then she leans back, the soft leather yielding beneath her head.

'Ashok?

'Ma'am?'

'I think I may as well just go along to the hotel right now.'

'So soon?'

'I guess I'm a little tired.'

'You are sure there is nothing else Ma'am?'

'No. That's fine—well, maybe just a question?'

'Ma'am—please ask it.'

'On my walk today, I went looking for the deer. But I couldn't find them. I didn't like to ask because, well, I guess, I didn't want to hear that they no longer keep deer in the Phoenix Park.'

'I can assure you, they certainly do. The deer, you see, congregrate in different areas depending on the time of day.'

'You sure about that? Because let me tell you, I don't need another let-down today.'

'Ma'am—I know that Phoenix Park like my own backyard.'

The car twists up along Military Road, past the Magazine Fort. Ashok considers turning into the first and smaller carpark; a cosy green haven where a few parked cars, a single man to each one, are always in situ. But he has heard rumours of what sometimes goes on in there and he doesn't want his VIP viewing more than the deer. He turns into the second, larger carpark and carefully brings the Mercedes to an angled stop. On one side, the playing fields, stretching pitch to pitch, into a deep-green distance. On the other side, the ugly grey block of the sports changing-rooms. To the front, the deer, arranged in quiet dun-coloured groups under the trees.

Mrs Ridell releases a sigh. 'They are so beautiful, ' she says. 'They are so—'

'Peaceful?' Ashok suggests, turning to see her small face peeping out at him from the gap between the seats. 'You know Ma'am, you would enjoy a clearer view of the deer, were you to sit up front.'

Mrs Riddel nods and Ashok moves his chauffeur's hat from the passenger seat and lays it on the dashboard, then comes around to the back door and helps her to move. The yellow handbag stays behind.

A light shower begins to fall, gradually coating the windscreen in a veil of rain. They sit in silence, watching the deer. After a time Mrs Ridell speaks, 'I don't recall the grass being so long, last visit.'

'Oh and it will get longer, Ma'am. The fawning season, you see, which is just now beginning. The grass is always longer during this time. Except for the playing fields which must remain clipped.'

'I like it long. It's—well, less contrived, I guess.'

'Or more natural, Ma'am.'

'Yes, or that.'

'It is at its most beautiful at daybreak, and then again, just before sunset. In these moments, the grasses turn pink at the tips. With the red of the sky and the push of the breeze, it's like the grass is painting the sky—you know? It's the most unusual thing I've seen since arriving here. Well, that and the silent traffic jam which I also find remarkable, but in a different way, of course.'

'How long have you been here, Ashok?'

'Oh, fifteen years or so.'

'You like it?'

'Oh yes, very much, Ma'am, thank you for asking. Well. No actually, not really. At least, not any more.'

'And do you have family here?'

Ashok looks away. After a moment he speaks, 'If you were to walk way out there to where the grass is longest, sooner or later you would hear the sound of a fawn crying. A most pitiful sound. And if you were to follow the sound you would find the poor creature all alone and huddled in the grass. The temptation of course would be to lift it up and carry it off to safety. But you must never do that.'

'No?'

'Oh no. No matter how much your heart may tell you to. Were you to touch it, the mother would then consider the fawn to be contaminated and she would abandon it.'

'I see,' Mrs Ridell says.

'The laws of nature are not always easy to understand,' Ashok hears himself mutter.

'Ashok—' she begins but he stops her with a smile and a lift of his hand.

'Oh, Ma'am, excuse me rambling on when I really meant to ask if you would care to have a cigarette here, in the car? Seeing as it's raining outside.'

'Why thank you. To have a cigarette sitting in comfort? I don't know when I last!'

He gets out of the car and pulls the handbag from the back seat.

'In your own home, Ma'am,' he says as he gets back in.

'Excuse me?'

'In your own home, you must enjoy in comfort, a cigarette.'

'Oh, yes, I see what you mean. But no. I've been pretty much living in hotels since my husband died.'

Mrs Ridell opens the bag and rummages until she finds first a lighter, then a pack of cigarettes, the cigarettes jammed in together and her fingers tugging like a bird at a worm in an effort to release one. Up close her hands look older.

Ashok takes the pack from her. He pulls out a cigarette and gives it to her, then he holds the lighter up. A perfect drop of fire. Mrs

Ridell pokes the tip of her cigarette into it and puffs. Ashok presses a button and her window purrs open.

'When I was a child,' he says. 'My mother had a yellow handbag.'

Mrs Ridell, puts her head to one side. 'Really?'

'Yes, a German lady gave it to her,' he says, 'my mother, you see, worked in the Taj Palace Hotel as a toilet cleaner. The most beautiful hotel in Bombay, she was most fortunate to have such a job.'

'I've heard of it, sure.'

'One day, my mother came across the German lady going into her room. The lady had dropped her key and my mother picked it up and opened the door for her. As she handed back the key, she saw that the woman was crying, sobbing in fact. She went into the room and stayed until the woman finally fell asleep. She never saw the woman again, although she remained several more days as a guest in the hotel. Nor did my mother ever know what it was that had made her cry so. After the woman had checked out, the head housekeeper came to my mother and handed her a brown paper parcel. Inside was the yellow handbag. My mother had noticed it in the lady's room and thought perhaps the lady had, in turn, noticed her admiring it.'

Ashok stops for a moment.

'Go on,' Mrs Ridell says.

'There is nothing to go on with,' Ashok says, turning to look out the window by his side. 'Except—'

'Yes?'

'When we were children, we thought she carried a piece of the sun around in that yellow handbag. Each time she opened it, something wonderful would emerge; small fragrant soaps, pieces of individually wrapped chocolate, pens and writing paper too, thick as cloth. A stick of kohl for my sisters' eyes, once a *Boy's Own Annual* for me! Such luxury was unheard of in our lives, so it was easy to believe the source would have to be magical. I realise now, of course, and with shame, that these things were stolen from the great Taj Hotel and that the sun had nothing to do with it.'

'But the yellow purse—that wasn't stolen.'

'Oh no, Ma'am. But neither did she own it. You see I believe a gift, a true gift must be accepted from the hand that gives it.'

Mrs Ridell tilts her chin towards the butt of her cigarette and takes one final pull before throwing it out the window. 'And your mother, Ashok? Is she still alive?'

'Oh yes, Ma'am. She is alive. Old, very old. In India.'

'And you—did you say you have family?'

Ashok slips the chauffeur's cap from the dashboard and begins to pick at its braided cord.

'Oh no, I have no one, Ma'am.'

'I see.'

'In a few weeks I will be seeing my mother in Bombay. Or Mumbai as I suppose we must call it now.'

'Well now! I suppose you're looking forward to that?'

'Oh yes, Ma'am. I suppose I am.'

'And will you return to Ireland? After your vacation, I mean?'

'Oh now, Ma'am,' he smiles, 'that is a very good question.'

He steps out of the car, perching the chauffeur's hat under his arm. 'We will go soon, Mrs Ridell,' he says, 'but if you would allow me a moment or two before setting off?'

Mrs Ridell nods.

He walks through flimsy rain across the cracks and bumps of the tarmacadam carpark, coming to a stop at the edge. A lone grazer has strayed from the herd and is plucking its way out from the trees towards the wide-open space of the playing field. Ashok watches it for a while, then slips his hand into his pocket. For a moment he hears the sounds of his childhood; boys' voices and the batting of cricket balls. He dips at the knee, and closing one eye, bowls his phone on a low daisy-cutter, over the grass.

NOTES ON THE AUTHORS

Colin Barrett is from Mayo. In 2009 he received the second annual Penguin Ireland Prize, awarded to the most promising fiction writer on the MA course in Creative Writing at University College Dublin. He received an Arts Council bursary in 2010. His fiction has appeared in *The Stinging Fly* and in the UCD anthology, *A Curious Impulse*.

Kevin Barry is the author of the story collection, *There Are Little Kingdoms*, and the forthcoming novel, *City Of Bohane*. His stories have appeared in *The New Yorker*, *The Stinging Fly*, *The Dublin Review* and many other journals and anthologies. He also writes film scripts and plays. He lives in County Sligo. He was awarded the Rooney Prize for Irish Literature in 2007.

Madeleine D'Arcy lives in Cork with her husband and son. She began writing fiction in 2005. In 2010 she was presented with a Hennessy Literary Award for First Fiction as well as the overall Hennessy New Irish Writer Award 2009.

Benjamin Arda Doty recently completed an MFA at the University of Minnesota. His short story here is an adaptation of a chapter from an as yet unpublished novel. His fiction has appeared in *Southword* and *Colorado Review*.

Alex Epstein was born in Saint Petersburg in 1971 and moved to Israel when he was eight years old. He is the author of three collections of short stories and three novels. In 2003 he was awarded Israel's Prime Minister's Prize for Literature. *Blue Has No South,* his most recent collection, is available in English, from Clockroot Books. [**Becka Mara McKay** is the author of the poetry collection, *A Meteorologist in the Promised Land,* and a translator from the Hebrew. Her recent translations include Suzane Adam's 'Laundry'. She is currently a professor of Creative Writing and Translation at Florida Atlantic University.]

Emily Firetog is from Brooklyn, New York, and is the former Assistant Editor of *The Stinging Fly*. She holds an MPhil in Creative Writing from Trinity College Dublin, was an Arts Council Bursary recipient in 2008, and was commended in the Sean O'Faolain Short Story competition in 2009. She is currently pursuing an MFA at Columbia University.

Marcus Fleming was raised in Kerry. An international career in animation led him to screenwriting, including for *The Running Mate,* which won the Best Drama category in the Irish Film and Television Awards in 2008. He lives in Dublin.

Andrew Fox was born in Dublin. A graduate of Trinity College's creative writing programme and an Arts Council bursary recipient in 2009, he has been shortlisted for a Hennessy Award and a Francis MacManus Award. He is currently pursuing a PhD in the United States.

Grace French lives in Dublin. She has worked as a lawyer and family mediator. A recent short story was shortlisted for the 2010 RTE Francis MacManus competition. She facilitates writing workshops using the AWA method.

Radu Pavel Gheo was born in 1969, in Romania, and has published nine books of fiction and essays, most recently the critically acclaimed novel *Good Night, Kids!*

Julian Gough was born in London, raised in Tipperary, educated in Galway, and now lives in Berlin. His novels are *Juno & Juliet* and *Jude: Level 1* (shortlisted for the Wodehouse Prize in 2008). *Free Sex Chocolate – Poems & Songs* was published by Salmon Poetry in 2010. He won the BBC National Short Story Award in 2007.

Charlotte Grimshaw is the author of four novels. She has won New Zealand's Buddle Findlay Sargeson Prize and the Katherine Mansfield Award. Her first story collection, *Opportunity*, was shortlisted for the Frank O'Connor Prize and won the Montana Fiction Award. Her second, *Singularity*, was shortlisted for the Frank O'Connor Prize and the Asia Pacific Commonwealth Writers' Prize.

Christine Dwyer Hickey has published five novels, most recently *Last Train from Liguria* (Atlantic Books, 2009). Twice winner of Listowel Writers' Week short story competition and a winner in the prestigious Observer/Penguin competition, her stories have appeared in various anthologies in Ireland and abroad. Her first collection will be published by New Island in 2011. She is a member of Aosdána.

Brian Kirk lives in Clondalkin, Dublin. He was shortlisted for Hennessy Awards in 2007 and 2010, and for the Over The Edge New Writer of the Year Awards in 2008 and 2009. He won the inaugural Writing Spirit Award in 2009. His stories have appeared in *The Sunday Tribune*, *Crannóg* and various anthologies.

Shih-Li Kow is a Malaysian writer who lives in Kuala Lumpur. Her collection, *Ripples and Other Stories*, was shortlisted for the 2009 Frank O'Connor Short Story Award. She is a chemical engineer but now works as a mall manager.

Gerry McCullough was born in North Belfast and has had over forty short stories published. Her novel, *Belfast Girls*, is to be published in the near future.

David Mohan is based in Dublin. He has been published in *The Sunday Tribune* and *Southword*. He came second in the 2009 Sean O'Faolain Short Story Award and won the 2009 Over The Edge Writer of the Year Award. He also won the Hennessy 2008 New Irish Writer Award.

Dónal Moloney is from Waterford. 'The Grind' is a short story version of the first chapter of a novella. He has been published in *Census: The First Seven Towers* Anthology. He works as a translator.

James Moynihan has published stories in a number of journals, won the Sean O'Faolain Prize and been placed in RTE's Francis MacManus competition.

Goran Petrović was born in 1961 in Serbia. He has published numerous novels and books of short stories over the past two decades and received many awards, including the 2000 NIN Literary Prize for his novel, *Sitničarnica 'Kod Srećne Ruke'* (*The Trinket Shop 'At the Lucky Hand'*), and the Andrić Award for his short story collection, *Razlike (Differences)*. His books have been translated into over a dozen languages. He lives in Belgrade with his wife and daughter. [**Peter Agnone** is the translator of the novel *Bait* by David Albahari (Northwestern University Press), as well as work by Goran Petrović, including the novel *The Trinket Shop 'At* *the Lucky Hand'* (Plato books). His translations of short fiction by numerous contemporary Serbian writers have appeared in Europe and America. He lives in Belgrade.]

Zakhar Prilepin served as a captain in a special unit on two deployments in Chechnya, in the 1990s. He started writing in 2004 and has since published a collection of short stories and a number of novels. He was awarded the Russian National Bestseller Award in 2008 for *Sin*. He is a journalist and anti-Putin activist and lives in Nizhny-Novgorod.

Luke Woods was born in northwestern Vermont and now lives in Brooklyn. His grandfather got into a fistfight with Ernest Hemingway in Paris just after WWII.

A NOTE ON THE EDITOR

Philip Ó Ceallaigh has published two collections of stories: *Notes from a Turkish Whorehouse* (2006), which won the Glen Dimplex New Writers Award for fiction, and *The Pleasant Light of Day* (2009). Both books were shortlisted for the Frank O'Connor International Short Story Award. Philip won the Rooney Prize for Irish Literature in 2006. He lives in Bucharest.

ACKNOWLEDGEMENTS

The editor would like to thank Oana Boca, Diana Chornenkaya, Fergal Condon, Patrick Cotter, Claire Coughlan, Vasile Ernu, Djordje Krivokapić, Declan Meade, Linda Murray, Hilary Plum, Alina Purcaru, Gabrielle Randle, Roman Simić and Bogdan Stanescu.